To
Charmain Zimmerman Brackett

# Murder en Pointe

Book 2

CHARMAIN Z. BRACKETT

DIAMOND KEY PRESS

Published October 2016, July 2018

Augusta is filled with so many amazing visual and performing artists. It makes the town a much more beautiful place to live. I want to dedicate this book to the many painters, dancers, musicians, and authors who make my hometown their hometown. You're all beautiful, and I want to say "thank you" for all you do. Of course, I'm biased. I'm the mom to three of the town's best dancers and the sister of Augusta's best and happiest visual artist.

# 1

"Jimmy Hughes, it hasn't even been a month yet. What are you doing in my shop?"

He smiled broadly before giving me a peck on the cheek. I laughed. Jimmy usually wiped my flower cases out once a month because he'd done something to upset his wife. That something often involved too much beer and a friendly poker game with a few of his buddies. But that was last week. He couldn't have done something again so quickly, could he?

"Aw, little lady, you've got it all wrong," Jimmy said in his thick Southern drawl. "This time, instead of getting me out of the dog house, you're going to keep me from being put in it."

"And how can I keep my best customer from going into the dog house?"

"Well, our anniversary is coming up. I'm even giving you a few days advance warning. I want something nice for her. Something real special."

"Anything in particular?"

"Well, you know how she loves the ballet and all that culture stuff. She's been going on and on about some Russian ballerina who's coming here. I have to take her to the performance for an anniversary present and then get her the same flowers that ballerina likes. Peggy said they're real pretty, and she wants some just like them. And that I better not screw it up."

The thought of Jimmy attending the ballet with Peggy made me laugh. I couldn't see it. Jimmy had been an auto mechanic all his life and owned a couple of repair shops. He was a little rough around the edges and had grease under his fingernails. His idea of dressing up was wearing a collared golf shirt with a pair of blue jeans and his cowboy boots. He was a likeable guy though, and he had a great sense of humor. And deep down, he really loved Peggy. I'd known them all of my life. They were longtime friends of my parents.

"Jimmy, I promise you won't screw it up if I have anything to do with it. I know exactly what and who you're talking about. Her name is Aleksandra something. I can barely pronounce her last name, much less spell it. She's with that Russian ballet group that is performing here next week, and they had me looking for some exotic orchids for her a couple of months ago. She has to have them in her dressing room. She claims that their scent calms her before her performance and brings her good luck. And if she doesn't have her flowers, she can't perform."

I waved my hands about trying to mimic a drama queen.

"Sounds like a diva to me," Emmie chimed in.

I laughed.

"Of course."

"Orchids," Jimmy snapped his fingers. "That's exactly what Peggy said she wanted."

"Jimmy, I have something similar coming in, but I'll let you know they are pricey. Some of the ones they wanted I can't even get here in the U.S. Fortunately, her publicists have been able to find substitutes without Aleksandra being any the wiser."

"Well, this is anniversary number 40. Those anniversaries ending in fives and zeroes are extra special from what I hear. Plus, I've got a special poker tournament coming up right after our anniversary. Some of my buddies from high school and me - we're getting together for a reunion. We do it at least once a year, and well, Peggy - she's never liked them. It may not end well."

I smiled at him and shook my head.

"Is it really worth the trouble, Jimmy?"

"Darn skippy, it is. Peggy is a lot of hot air, but she's my hot air. There's no bite to go along with that bark of hers. I love her, and she puts up with me," he said and winked.

"Sounds like true love," Emmie said.

"Are you giving her anything else besides flowers?"

"I have something for her that sparkles too."

"For 40 years of putting up with you, she needs more than flowers. I hope it sparkles a lot."

I winked at him when I said that.

"Oh yes, it sparkles a whole lot. It's a diamond tennis bracelet that I'm hoping sparkles enough that I don't have to see you too much in the next few weeks, Grace. No offense because you sure are pretty to look at," he said.

He laughed and leaned in to give me one final quick peck on the cheek.

"You know, it's those pecks on the cheek that you give the ladies that get you in trouble with Peggy."

He laughed and winked again.

"You always do well by me, Grace. There hasn't been a doghouse in a couple of years that one of your flower arrangements didn't get me out of. Besides the best part of the fighting is the making up afterwards anyway."

He winked at me, and I shook my head at him.

"And I know you won't disappoint me now," he said.

"I'll do my best. Would you like to see a photo?"

"A photo of what?"

"The flowers?"

"If you can fool the Russian ballerina, you can fool Peggy, and that's all I need," he said as he headed toward the door. "You've got my number. When you get a total, just call me. You should have my card number on file. Just charge it. I trust you."

Emmie shook her head and folded her arms as her eyes followed Jimmy.

"Those two make quite the pair," she said laughing.

"Yes, they do. They've always been that way though."

I turned and looked at her.

"What are you doing here today? You're supposed to be off."

"I love it when you do that, Grace. You always know how to make a girl feel wanted."

She gave me a broad smile when she said that.

"I'm sorry. I didn't mean -"

"I know you didn't, honey. I was just picking on you. You need to lighten up some."

She put her hand on my shoulder.

"Well, you don't usually come to work on your day off for no reason at all."

"That's true, but you are my best friend, and I had this feeling you needed me."

I tried to smile.

"Miss Grace, we have an order for a baby arrangement, but I need some stargazer lilies. We are slap out of them," said a Cajun-twanged voice.

"Look in the back case, Jazzy."

"That's where Grace hides things when she knows Jimmy Hughes is coming in," said Emmie.

She turned and looked at me.

"I need to talk to you - in private."

"Not a problem."

I wondered what was coming next. Emmie didn't have problems talking to me in front of anyone. Emmie led the way to my office and sat down at my desk. She clasped her hands in her lap and fidgeted.

"Grace, I think what you are doing for Jazzy is a wonderful thing. You're a good person, and that's the reason you're doing it."

"We're all helping Jazzy out of a bad situation. Someone had to. She had nowhere to turn, and I didn't want to see her going back to Atlanta to live on the streets."

"I know."

"Besides, if Beth hadn't offered the loft above their detached garage as a place for Jazzy to live, I couldn't have done my part in all of this. Jazzy's not making a lot of money. She helps Beth out some after the regular nanny goes home at night. I think Beth is helping Jazzy more than any of us."

"Don't sound like you're apologizing to me. I know she's not making much, but I know you really can't afford both of us and Beth too."

"Things have been a lot better, and we've got so many weddings coming up this summer. Look, Emmie, I'm going to make this work. You don't have to worry about it. I will keep you as busy as you want to be. Besides, Jimmy Hughes keeps me afloat most months."

Emmie started to respond but stopped and stared at me for a minute. She shook her head.

"Grace Ward, what do you know that you aren't telling me?"

"What are you talking about, Emmie?"

"Don't lie to me, Grace. What did you want to tell me?"

I had no idea what she was talking about as she stared at me. I shook my head slowly as I tried to think of something to say. She simply stared at me and waited. All of a sudden, a dream I'd had a few nights before flooded my mind. I hadn't deliberately withheld it. I had gotten sidetracked, and it slipped my mind. I didn't mean to, but I gasped. She raised her eyebrow and nodded at me.

"See. You are keeping something."

"Oh, no. I'm so sorry."

"I knew it. I knew you weren't telling me something."

"How did you know?"

"You aren't the only one who knows stuff, you know."

"Well, I had a dream about you a couple of nights ago. I guess I'd forgotten about it until now. I haven't seen you in a couple of days, and Jazzy has kept me on my toes getting her ready to go to Augusta Tech and all. She's got a lot of energy. I've never met anyone with that much energy."

Emmie laughed.

"True. She's a ball of fire. I love having her around, but you are avoiding my question. What aren't you telling me?"

I'd gotten distracted again. It had been happening a lot. I couldn't focus. I had so many things on my mind. I sat down at my desk, trying to piece it together. I didn't tell Emmie? How did that happen?

"Sorry, you wanted to hear about my dream. I can't believe I didn't call you. I'm not sure where my head has been."

She nodded.

"I've wondered that too. You haven't been my friend, Grace, since the murder right before the tournament. I don't know where you've been, and it scares me that I don't know how to reach you. I see glimmers sometimes, but then you disappear again."

I didn't know what to say to that so I just blurted out the dream, hoping to distract her.

"My dream wasn't much. I saw you wearing an ID badge on the lapel of a blazer and drawing in a sketch pad."

"And?"

"You were wearing a suit. You never wear suits, and this one was so ugly, so not Emmie."

We both laughed.

"No, I hate suits, and you ignored my comment earlier," she paused. When I didn't say anything, she let out an exaggerated sigh. I knew she was frustrated with me. "Just keep going with the dream."

"You were sketching faces, like a police sketch artist."

Emmie leaned back in the chair and took a deep breath. Then, she smiled.

"I wasn't sure what I was supposed to do. Now, I know," she said.

"What are you talking about?"

"When did you have this dream?"

"Just a few days ago. Saturday night after the Palmer-Ferguson wedding. But on Sunday, my brother was in town, and we had that family get together. That was hard."

"Well, I got a call about a week ago from Special Agent Frank Monroe with the FBI. He told me there was a temporary position open. They need someone like me to work as a sketch artist and do some computer things. It's sort of on an on-call, as-needed basis to fill in gaps when people aren't available. I'd cover cases in a two-hour radius of Augusta."

"Emmie, that sounds amazing."

"It does, but I've thought about my kids. I'd have to travel, and I might have to leave them more than I want."

"Where's my adventuresome best friend?"

She smiled as she looked down at her hands. I wasn't sure what was wrong or why she was so nervous.

"We've switched places in the past couple of months, Grace, remember?"

I smiled.

"Anyway, Drew also mentioned that the sheriff's department might be interested in me as well. I've already talked with them some. They might call me for a trial run so to speak."

"I've always thought you were incredible, Emmie. You don't give your talent and your artwork enough credit."

She looked up at me.

"I could still work around here too," she said in a sheepish tone.

"Weren't you trying to quit a minute ago? Emmie, you've got to do what's best for you. I don't want to hold you back in any way. I've always wanted you to pursue your art, and I keep telling you I want to make space for your artwork here. We could do an exhibit or something. You know Beth would love to cater a reception. I wish you'd take me up on it."

"I know. I like it here with you. I guess I'm comfortable here. I never thought I'd get comfortable. That means I'm old and settled in my ways," she said as she shook her head. "I like flowers. I like having people smile at me because the flowers I designed made their wedding more special or made their dinner party more beautiful."

"I feel the same way, and I certainly wouldn't hold it against you if you wanted to show up here and make arrangements. But I would never want to be the reason you didn't go after a career doing something you loved. What kind of friend does that?"

"And you're right. Let's have an art exhibit. A big one, in a couple of months. We'll let Beth show off too. I'll buy canvas and paint, and we'll do this."

I smiled.

"That's my Emmie."

"Oh and keep some wedding arrangements open for me. I'm not sure how this will turn out."

"When do you need to let them know something?"

"Within the next week or so."

"Good. You'll still be here to help me with the prima ballerina."

"Did you find her orchids?"

"Yes, and I ordered extra. There are two performances and then there's a sponsor party. We're making the arrangements for the party too. Since Aleksandra is the star, I have to include some of her signature orchids in the pieces I make for the party."

"This is exciting. I always loved ballet."

"Me too. We had so much fun taking ballet together as kids. But let's face it - my name might be 'Grace,' but I don't live up to it - in a tutu that is. I wish I could've danced longer, but too many ankle sprains ended it for me. I think I spent more time on crutches than at the barre."

Emmie laughed.

"My talent is with a sketchbook or a piece of canvas, but I've always admired performers. And I think we both sprained our ankles before one recital."

"I remember that. It wasn't ballet's fault though. You and I were horsing around."

She nodded.

"Guilty."

As quickly as she smiled, Emmie got serious and furrowed her brow at me.

"What's the matter, Emmie?"

"As much as I love flowers, there was something about helping Drew with that case, even if I just played a small part. It was exciting."

I tried not to laugh.

"It was exciting, but not in the right way. Dead bodies and all."

"But knowing you've made a difference..."

I nodded. I guess I'd made a difference. They said I did. I just couldn't shake the bad memories. It was like Emmie guessed what was going through my mind. She put her hand out to touch mine.

"You did make a difference," she whispered.

I nodded.

"The idea of leaving you and what I know is scary too, but in a different way," said Emmie. "But the idea of something new is definitely exciting."

"Stop it. It's not like you're dying or anything like that. You're my best friend. I'll still be here for you."

Emmie stood up and came around to my desk to give me a big hug.

"We should still be able to have girls' nights every now and then."

"Agreed."

# 2

I headed toward the William B. Bell Auditorium, an Art Moderne structure completed in 1940 and named after a former mayor, with my specific instructions in hand. Flowers were to be set up in her dressing room a certain way, down to the exact measurements of how far away they needed to be from the mirror. There would be several arrangements in the dressing room. There was one mix of orchids with no other flowers; there were one dozen lavender roses in a cut crystal vase; and there was one orchid bloom alone in a champagne glass filled with champagne of course. The roses had to be embellished with sequins. Yes, sequins. I was glad this paid well. Apparently, a wealthy arts patron ponied up to have this group come to town and was aware of the extra cost of having to deal with the diva.

The flowers had to be fresh and placed in the dressing room no more than an hour before she arrived. She claimed their scent was at a maximum level then and any less scent would affect her performance. I had a feeling this dancer wasn't too bright, knowing how long it took to get these items in. It wasn't like anyone could just go pick these exotic orchids and bring them into her dressing room. Still, I tried to abide by her guidelines as much as possible.

I had a meeting with someone in theater management to discuss the delivery procedure on the day of the first performance.

"You have the instructions?" he asked as he led me to the dressing rooms.

I held up a printout of the email I received.

"I'm ready. I even brought my tape measure because I know she wants her roses a certain distance from the orchids."

"Yes, I've heard she breaks things if everything isn't in order, and we can't have that. She's broken mirrors and chairs in other places she's performed."

He led me to her dressing room and knocked.

"She's on stage, but just in case," he said.

He paused, and when there was no reply, we entered. I looked at her makeup and dressing area. Everything was in order according to the diagram I'd been emailed, making it easier to arrange the flowers as specified. I made a few notes on my printout, and I took a couple of photos. I glanced around the dressing room. I saw several costume bags hanging in the room. There was one costume out of its bag. It had a gorgeous white bodice bedecked in the most amazing rhinestones I'd ever seen. I had to resist the urge to touch it. It was stunning. I rotated again and looked at her counter space. There was a lovely tiara in a clear, plastic box at the far end of the counter away from her make-up and away from where I was supposed to put the flowers.

"Wow, a ballerina with a temper, and they look so beautiful on stage."

"Yes, she's both beautiful and angry. That combination could be dangerous, and other theaters have definitely felt the brunt of it."

"What does she do if everything isn't to her liking?"

"She typically throws the closest object at someone's head. Fortunately, for most people, she's a dancer not a baseball player."

He did not laugh as he said that so I had to resist the urge, but it wasn't easy.

"Has she ever hit anyone?"

He nodded at me.

"Only one or two, but crystal vases against the skull can be pretty nasty. And she shows no signs of remorse."

"How nice."

He shook his head.

"Do you have everything you need?" he asked.

I nodded, and we headed out of the dressing room. I could hear music coming from inside the theater. It was the music the Little Swans danced to in Tchaikovsky's Swan Lake. I remembered it from when my mother took me to see it in Atlanta one time. I danced around for weeks after that, pretending to hold hands with my swan partners. I forced my mother to order a copy of it for me from a local music store.

"They're having a rehearsal before the show tonight. Their artistic director and ballet mistress are slave drivers. They'll have a two-hour rehearsal then there's more dancing before the performance tonight."

"I guess watching a rehearsal is forbidden."

"Some performers don't mind if there are people in the theater, but this group doesn't even want us back here in the dressing rooms."

I could hear the music make a sudden stop as an angry female voice spoke out in Russian.

The manager looked at me.

"Something tells me someone is not happy."

It wasn't hard to hear the shouting. It was a man and a woman, and even though I didn't know Russian, even I could tell they were arguing. Their words were loud and sharp and uttered in clipped tones.

"I will agree with you on that. I'll just duck out before they know I'm here. I'll be back at 6:30?"

It was more of a question than a statement because I wasn't sure exactly when I should show back up. That was left out of the instructions.

"Yes, that will be fine. You'll have a brief window of time while she's on-stage warming up. Don't miss your window. She won't want you in her dressing room. She wants to think the flower fairies decorated while she was gone."

I wasn't sure if he was serious or if that was a joke. He didn't laugh and kept a straight face as he said it. In fact, he had a straight face the entire time. He showed no emotion.

"Oh and for tomorrow, I found out she needs an orchid and rose arrangement before her rehearsal."

"Okay. I think I have enough orchids and roses. Do you have anything more specific?"

"Please say you do, and no, I don't have anything more specific. Maybe you can follow the guidelines you've already been given. Don't deviate from the pattern."

He sounded half hopeful, half desperate.

"I ordered extra."

"Thank you; thank you. You know, I called several florists in town before I found someone who would deal with this picky of a customer. I'm so glad I found you."

It looked like he tried to smile on that one. I wasn't sure, but I smiled anyway.

As we stood in the hallway of the dressing room area, several leotard-clad ballerinas walked passed us. They seemed to be mumbling to each other, and they weren't happy. A couple of them had tears streaming down their cheeks. I guess it wasn't two people arguing after all, but two people handing out criticism toward the dancers.

"I think that's my cue to leave."

He nodded. As we stood there, another dancer walked passed us and said something in Russian in a disgusted tone. She glared dead at me and narrowed her eyebrows at me as though she didn't want me in her way. She had red hair. I wondered if this was the diva ballerina.

"Don't forget your window of opportunity this evening. Someone will be here to let you in," he said. He turned and walked away.

I started to head for the door. I went for the keys in my pocket, but they weren't there. What had I done with them? I stood there, patting my pockets and mentally retracing my steps. I knew that I had them when I came in. I wondered if I'd put them down in the dressing room when I was making notes? I need to go back in there. That would mean encountering the diva, but I couldn't wait until their break was over.

I walked back to the dressing room and knocked. I heard a flood of Russian I didn't understand.

"I'm sorry. I don't understand Russian," I yelled from the other side.

A perplexed ballerina opened the door. She was petite. She couldn't have been more than 5 feet tall. She was wearing a black leotard with spaghetti straps and pink tights with thick pink leg warmers over them. Her brown hair was slicked back into a perfect bun. She cocked her head to the side as she stared at me. She was hot and sweaty. Although she didn't have an ounce of makeup on, she was beautiful. Her skin was so clear. And there she stood with a bottle of water in her hand. This was the diva I'd heard so much about? She wasn't what I'd envisioned at all. I had been so busy lately. I didn't do any research on the ballet company. I supposed I should have - at least for curiosity's sake, but I didn't. If she was the diva, who was the redhead?

"I think I left my keys in here. I apologize," I explained.

She stood back and let me in without saying anything. She didn't seem annoyed or angry that I was invading her dressing room. She was just confused.

"I'm the florist. I was just getting some final instructions for your dressing room when I left my keys here."

"Ah. You are bringing the orchids?"

She smiled. That surprised me after all the horror stories I'd heard. She had beautiful eyes. They were brown with gold flecks in them, and they sparkled when she talked. I wasn't one who was drawn to people's eyes. I usually didn't notice unless they stared at me for a long time.

"Yes. That's what I was told you wanted."

"Do not believe everything any of these people tell you," she said. Her English was perfect but formal sounding. She spoke with only a slight Russian accent. She had a lovely, lilting voice. That surprised me too. She wasn't the angry diva I'd heard so much about. She was pleasant.

"Really?"

"Don't get me wrong. I do love orchids. They are beautiful, but they are so expensive - such a waste. I liked the lavender roses the best, but the sparkles on them are too much. This orchid charade is Vladimir's doing."

"Vladimir?"

"He's the artistic director. He created this madness around me."

"I'm sorry to have bothered you."

"No, you are not bothering me at all. It's nice to talk to someone," she paused and drank some more water.

I stared at her. I didn't understand.

"All of this masquerade has separated me from the other dancers. They think I'm a," she paused and snapped her fingers. "I cannot think of your English word."

"Diva?" I offered timidly.

She laughed.

"Ah, yes, diva. It's a silly image. I do not understand, but it helps publicity, according to Vladimir. Publicity is good, but it makes for a lonely life on the road. The stories they tell about me. I've heard them all. Crystal vases thrown at people's heads and shouting matches. Orchids in champagne. I feel like a circus attraction. 'Come see the evil diva.' The only thing I want is to dance and give a beautiful performance."

She looked away as she said that. Her lilting tone dropped to a sad note.

"I do have some lovely orchids for you, and yes, I have a lot of the lavender roses as well."

I didn't know how to cheer her up.

"Spasibo," she said and smiled at me.

I shook my head.

"It's Russian for 'thank you.'"

"If you don't mind me asking, what are your favorite flowers?"

She smiled.

"Sunflowers. They are happy flowers with big, beautiful faces. And they remind me of home."

I totally did not see that coming. I agreed. I always thought sunflowers were happy flowers too. Yellow was always a happy color - so bright and cheerful. And the Russian mammoth variety of sunflowers could indeed grow to massive sizes.

"I'll see that you get some sunflowers. I don't have any of the Russian variety though, and my keys are right over there. I'll be back soon."

"Spasibo. You are too kind to me. I wish I could meet more people like you, but they only see the sideshow act and keep their distance from me. I would love a sunflower. Now, you must excuse me, I have to get back on the stage. My water break is over," she said, grabbing another bottle of water as she passed me on the way out.

I followed her and stood at the door, peering out onto the stage. She took a position away from the other dancers. She seemed so lonely. How sad for her. The dancers were taking a break. Some of them sat on the floor and stretched while others talked among themselves. Some didn't even notice as Aleksandra walked past them; some even turned their backs as she passed. I watched as a man clapped his hands and said something in Russian. I guess that was their cue to start again. He waved his hand, and the dancers fell into a pattern. With another wave of his hand, the music began, and someone closed the door on my intrusion.

"Well, I guess that's that," I said into the silence.

I stared at the door for a few moments. It was hard to believe that that woman was the terror she'd been made out to be. I questioned the story I'd heard earlier about throwing those cut crystal vases at people's heads and being angry over flower arrangements. I didn't believe it for a second. Why would they tell such stories? I thought it was a strange type of publicity stunt.

Oh how, I wanted to see the performance, but Drew didn't like ballet, and Emmie had her kids. Beth had said she wasn't going. I didn't want to go by myself. I put those thoughts out of my head as I dashed back to the shop. I needed to make sure the orchids looked their best for tonight, and I had to embellish the extra lavender roses with small rhinestones even though she said she didn't care for them. They were part of the order that someone had generously paid for.

I looked at the clock. It was approaching closing time so I didn't expect too many more customers on the day. I'd sent Jazzy home and was putting the final touches on the evening's flowers when I heard the bell ring. Drew had made sure someone fixed the bell, and it was really loud.

There was a young man at the counter. He fidgeted as he looked down at a piece of paper he held in his hands.

"Hi, I have an order for you," he said, glancing at me. He wrinkled his brow and scratched his head. "It's for Aleksandra, and I -"

"Can't pronounce the last name?"

We both laughed as he nodded.

"I know who you are talking about."

"Do you have sunflowers and lavender roses? I've been a couple of places that had the sunflowers, but no lavender roses."

"Yes, I have them both. What exactly do you need?"

"I have it written down. Sunflowers and a dozen lavender roses wrapped in white -" he paused and showed me the card pointing to the word "tulle."

"Yes, I have tulle."

"I have another card with the message written on it. It's in a foreign language. I don't know what it says. I just work at the hotel where this guy is staying. "

He handed me a 3-inch by 5-inch card.

"No problem. I'm going to the theater tonight. I'll take these to her."

"Can you get it there by 5:30?

That was cutting it close. It was almost 4:30 now and an hour before I was supposed to get there. But the theater wasn't that far from my shop so it wasn't that big of a deal.

"Sure. That's not a problem."

"Thanks."

I glanced at the card it was written on. It was typed out in Russian. So much for figuring out what our admirer wanted to say. There was no name listed.

"It's not signed."

"Yeah. I thought that was weird too, but that's the way he wanted it."

"I get weird requests all the time. I'll get them there."

I told him how much it was, and he handed me much more than it cost.

"I can't keep all of this. It's way too much."

"He said to consider it a tip. He gave me a big one too."

The courier had a big smile when he said that.

I stared at the card.

Lavender roses wrapped in white tulle and sunflowers. I had extra. Interesting that those were the two flowers she said she loved the most, and no mention of orchids which were supposedly her calling card. This person knew Aleksandra. I wondered about the sender. I wondered if I should put the card with the arrangement as it was. I liked to hand write the cards though. I thought it added a personal touch. I decided to try my hand at writing in Russian. I could copy it.

I quickly got the flowers together and a little before 5 o'clock, I headed to the theater. I was early, but I needed to get these flowers to their destination per my customer's request. I made my way to the back stage door because the box office was already closed. I noticed it was ajar; something was stuck in the door to keep it open. I thought that was a little strange because I expected a person to open the door for me.

With the arrangement in one hand, I opened the door and glanced around the inside of the theater. I walked around and listened.

Silence - an eerie silence, at that.

I seemed to be alone, but for some reason, I felt like someone was watching me. I felt a shiver down my spine. I'd never heard of a phantom at this theater. I felt the urge to get out of there as fast as I could. I wanted to run.

I put my hand on the door handle and paused as I felt another shiver. That urge to run was even stronger. I knocked on the door and waited. Despite the feeling of dread, I opened the door, and what I saw as I entered the dressing room shocked me. I saw a woman lying on her back on the floor. It was Aleksandra. Wearing a beautiful, silk, Asian-inspired robe, the same leotard and tights from earlier, and a pair of pink pointe shoes on her feet, she lay motionless.

I stepped back and paused for what seemed like an eternity. Of course, it was probably only a few seconds. I couldn't scream, but my heart felt like it was going to beat out of my chest. When I finally got my bearings, I placed the flowers on the makeup counter in front of the wall of mirrors and then stared into the reflection. There was something written in Russian in red lipstick on one of the dressing room mirrors. Another mirror was broken and several of the light bulbs that surrounded it were broken as well. Bloodied glass shards lay on the counter and pulverized purple eye shadow glittered on the floor. Several containers littered the carpet as though Aleksandra had entered a massive struggle right before her violent end.

I noticed a second pair of pointe shoes beside her. Saturated in blood, the shoes' ribbons were laced around her neck, and orchid blossoms were scattered atop her still body. There was blood on her hands, which were resting by her side. It was odd. It didn't seem like a natural position. My own hands started shaking as I took it all in. I felt dizzy. Where was my phone? I rummaged through my purse until I found it. Speed dial 2 for my husband.

"Hey, baby. I was just getting ready to call you," I heard Drew on the other end of the call.

I continued to stare.

"Grace? Are you there?"

"Drew" was all I could say.

"What's wrong?"

"Could you come to the dressing rooms at the Bell?"

The words seemed to be stuck in my throat. I tried to clear it.

"What's the matter, Grace?"

"I think there's been another murder."

"I'm on my way."

I stood paralyzed, transfixed on that face. The last dead body I'd seen wasn't looking back at me. Of course, I wasn't standing as close to her as I was standing to this body. I wanted to touch her, to shake her, to make her move. I wanted her to be asleep and dreaming - not dead. Anything but dead. I wanted her to open her eyes and talk to me. She could've even yelled at me in Russian - anything would have been better than this. I shook my head. This couldn't be happening again. I was looking into Aleksandra's face. She was the same woman who I chatted with only a few hours before. I could still see the sparkle in her eyes. I could see her beautiful smile and the kind way she spoke. She was so different from the picture that people painted of her. And now, she was dead. Was her image what got her killed? I had a hard time wrestling with the two images. She seemed like such a nice person.

I knew not to touch anything at the crime scene. I didn't want to contaminate any evidence, but I guess I already had just by being here. When I told Drew I'd help him on another case, I'd only been kidding around, at least I thought I'd been kidding. I'd remembered a heart cry to want to be more in my husband's world, but this is not how I thought that request would be answered. This wasn't the part of his world I was talking about, but then again, this was a huge part of his world. I was still holding my phone. My hands were shaking. For some strange reason that I couldn't quite grasp, I began to snap a few photographs of the mirror and the scene. I even took pictures of the body. Drew would kill me if he knew I did that. But what he didn't know wouldn't hurt him. I was in this part of his world now; maybe I could help him again. I tried to compose myself and take in as much of the crime scene as I could. I wanted to have a level head. I was going to have to give a statement, and I needed to remember everything even the details such as the aroma of the orchids mixed with the scent of hairspray and sweat. Someone had said she thought the orchids brought her good luck. Apparently not this time.

I couldn't do it though - be strong and level-headed, that is. I wasn't cut out for this. My knees buckled beneath me. I stepped backward then fell to the floor. I scooted back until I felt the wall pressed against me. I didn't want to sit too close to the body, but I was too weak in the knees to walk out of the room. The only time I'd ever been this close to a dead body was at a couple of funerals. I tried not to get too close to bodies even then. The more I looked at her, the more I wondered if she was real. The image of the vivacious young woman from just a few hours ago was fading. That was the picture I wanted to see, but I couldn't replace that image with the one that was before me. I noticed her face and her eyes. There were tiny red dots on them. I'd watched too many crime shows - so that's what petechial hemorrhaging looked like. I was starting to feel nauseated. My mind was all over the place.

Where was Drew? I looked at my phone. It had been only three minutes since I called him, but it seemed like it had been hours.

Why hadn't I dreamed about this? Or had I? All I could remember was tossing and turning at night trying to get images of a dead woman floating in the Savannah River out of my head. Those pictures didn't want to go away. In the weeks since that first murder, I could block out the memory during the day, but at night, it resurfaced. I don't think I'd dreamed much of anything else. I tried not to sleep at all, and it was wearing on me. The dream of Emmie was the only other one I remembered. Pointe shoes, flowers, tutus, dance - none of these had come up and certainly not a new corpse.

As I sat there staring at her face, I heard a commotion in the hallway. I prayed it was Drew, and it was. I could hear him calling my name. I tried to stand with my legs still shaking and opened the door to alert him to where I was. He touched my arm and gave me a quick smile before going to look at the body. There were medical people and then I saw someone wearing a jacket with coroner written on it as well as a few deputies crammed into the tiny dressing room. I moved into the hallway away from the body. I tried to catalog all of those who'd entered the room. I hoped seeing a dead body wasn't going to become a regular occurrence. I didn't think I could get used to it. I felt ill, and it was hot in this backstage area. I rushed into the bathroom next to Aleksandra's dressing room. I had to throw up.

After a few minutes of sitting on the cold tile floor, I started to cry. Two beautiful young lives snuffed out in the past few months. I walked over to the sink. I rinsed out my mouth and splashed some cold water on my face. I glanced into the mirror. I was pale. I took a deep breath. Drew was going to be looking for me to give that statement to another deputy. I needed to get ready. I opened the door to find a congested backstage area. I noticed one of the stage doors had been propped open. I didn't recall an open door when I entered the theater from the outside. I walked into the wings of the darkened stage and stood there in the silence.

"Grace?"

I heard Drew calling my name and stepped back into the cramped hallway, where he was waiting for me. He pulled me close to him, and I rested my head against his chest, trying to fight the urge to cry.

"Mrs. Ward, what are you doing at my crime scene - again?" he whispered into my ear. His tone was light-hearted, and he laughed after saying it. I knew he was trying to make me laugh, but I couldn't. I still felt light-headed and nauseated.

He stepped back and stared into my eyes. He gently touched my cheek.

"Are you okay? You don't look so great. I mean, you're

beautiful, but you're as white as a sheet."

I wasn't sure how to answer that.

"I just threw up."

"I'm surprised you didn't do that last time. It's a common reaction. You know the drill. I'm going to need to get a statement from you."

I nodded. My mind was swirling, and then I remembered the reason I'd arrived at the theater so early.

"You need to come back to my shop with me. I have some evidence for you there."

"As soon as everything is cleared here, I'll head that way," he said.

"I think it's important, Drew."

He nodded.

"I trust you, but let me get this under control here first, baby."

"Take some deep breaths. It's going to be okay. I'll be back as soon as I can."

He walked to another deputy and brought him toward me.

"You need to give him your statement, Grace. Try to tell him as many details as you can remember."

Then he turned to the deputy.

"Would you take her outside this area and let her sit on the stairs? I'm not sure she's okay to stand right now."

The deputy nodded, and Drew walked back into the dressing room. I had the picture of everything burned into my brain as well as in my phone. We walked out of the dressing room area and sat on the stairs.

"Are you okay, ma'am?" he asked.

I nodded although I wasn't sure everything was okay. There was so much going on. I just wanted to get away from all of it. I wasn't cut out to be a detective. I was a florist. I gave my statement. This time around, I think I remembered more than I forgot. At least, I hope I did. I told the officer everything I could. I even told him about the messenger and the flowers and that Drew said he'd follow up with that.

It wasn't long before the theater management had shown up along with some bewildered Russians. The deputies cordoned off an area for the dancers. They needed to ask them questions as well. I wished I knew Russian. I would've loved to have understood what they were saying amongst themselves. A couple of them fixed their eyes on me and then began walking my way.

"You found her?" one of the dancers asked in a thick Russian accent.

"Yes."

"How did she die? Was it slow and painful?"

She had thick red hair, and her green eyes were cold as she stared at me waiting for a response. I remembered her. She was the one who'd glared at me earlier in the day.

"I don't know. I can't really talk about it."

She mumbled something in Russian to the petite blonde dancer standing beside her. "Natasha, now's your chance. You can be the star," the blonde replied in English as she placed her bony hand on Natasha's arm.

Natasha shook her head.

"This means nothing. Vladimir only had eyes for Aleksandra. Besides, he thinks I am fat."

I wanted to laugh. I don't think either of them knew the meaning of the word "fat." If they were fat, then I was morbidly obese. They looked like poster children for those hunger relief programs you see on late night TV.

Out of the corner of my eye, I noticed Drew coming out of the dressing room area. He raised an eyebrow at me as he approached. I could tell he didn't want me talking to these women.

"Excuse me, ladies. We need to get some information from you."

They mumbled in Russian as he moved them away. I reached out for his arm, and he looked at me.

"Drew, I need you to come to my shop. I have something

there."

He nodded as I pleaded with him, but he was soon interrupted again.

"Officer, I am Vladimir, the company's artistic director," said a short, balding man. He had a thick Russian accent. I recognized his voice as one of the people who was shouting earlier. "We have a performance in less than two hours."

Drew shook his head.

"I'm sorry, sir, but this is a crime scene now."

Vladimir looked confused.

"What do you mean 'crime scene?'"

"There's a dead body in the dressing room. There's not going to be a performance here tonight. No one is allowed back in that area."

"You do not understand. We have large group from Atlanta here to see the dancers. Atlanta has a huge Russian population. They want to see the dancers of their homeland."

"I'm sorry. We have to investigate a death and having an extra 2,000 people here isn't going to help. You'll have to postpone it. This scene won't be clear in time."

I continued to watch Vladimir's face. I thought it was odd that he was having no reaction whatsoever to the news that there'd been a murder in the theater. Then in an instant his face changed. He must not have understood what Drew was saying.

"Dead body?" he asked.

Drew nodded.

A shocked look broke across Vladimir's face. He broke down and began to weep and not quietly either.

"Who was it?" he asked.

Drew was silent. Vladimir looked around as though he was trying to figure out who was missing, then he turned toward to the doors to the dressing room area.

"Aleksandra? No, no. Anyone but Aleksandra."

Drew still said nothing. Vladimir threw up his hands in a

desperate motion as he moaned in Russian, and the emotion got the better of him. He fell on his knees and began to weep. An older woman came over to him and put her arm around him. I'd heard them talk about the ballet mistress. I wondered if that's who she was. Her hair was in a bun like most of the other dancers, but it was a fuller bun with silver threads running through her black hair. She had on a lot of mascara and eye makeup. Crying would've made quite a mess. She helped him up and pulled him out of the way.

I tried to move away from the scene, from Drew, from all of this. I felt claustrophobic, and I didn't like conflict. The idea of throwing up again started to return. I retreated up the staircase I'd been sitting on and headed toward a quiet spot on another set of stairs leading to the balcony seats. I sat on the floor wanting this second nightmare to end. As I stared at a blank wall, I took a few deep breaths. Away from the throng, my head started to clear a little even though I could still hear the rumble of voices below me.

Somehow, this seemed vaguely familiar. Deja vu? That feeling I'd get when I'd dreamt about something. Although I knew I'd never seen them, I thought I recognized the faces of the dancers. There was something about the orchids too. I couldn't put my finger on it. I ran through my recent dreams in my head, recalling what I'd told Emmie a few days before. I thought about seeing her drawing in a sketchbook. She was obviously working on a case, but what else was in the dream?

I recalled what she was wearing in the dream. I remembered that vividly. It wasn't Emmie-like at all. Even though she was on a budget, she managed to dress well. She loved to look at magazines to pull off the latest trends or just do whatever she wanted. She liked to mix and match styles, and somehow she could pull it off. She wore cowboy boots with dresses and stiletto heels with tight blue jeans and shirts with vibrant patterns or soft, flowing sleeves. She wore vintage clothes one day and something that looked off the most recent runway the next. She was unpredictable. She wore whatever she felt like, and in my shop, it didn't matter. No matter what she wore, it was always in good taste. In my dream, she wore a suit - an ugly suit and ugly shoes. I think people would call them functional shoes, but to Emmie, they would have been atrocious. Could the dream have had to do with this case? Emmie had told me that she was going to follow up with both Drew and Agent Monroe about the jobs, but she hadn't given me any updates.

I took a deep breath and tried to remember what else was in the dream. It hadn't been that long since I'd had it. Surely I could remember more of it. Sometimes when I focused on the bits I remembered, the rest came flooding back.

"God, help me remember."

It was just a whisper as I closed my eyes and fixed on the image of Emmie in a suit and holding a sketchpad. But I didn't see anything else. The noise from the theater pierced through my thoughts with one voice standing out from the rest. It sounded like Emmie. I looked around. I knew I had vivid dreams, but this was a little too real. I strained my ears. Yes. It was definitely Emmie's voice coming from downstairs. She could be loud when she needed to be. After all, she was the mother of two little boys. What was she doing here? My curiosity got the better of me, and I walked down the stairs. I peeked around the corner, and there she was.

"Just ask Investigator Drew Ward. I'm supposed to be here. He's the one who called me."

She stood there with her sketchbook in hand and wearing the exact suit I saw in the dream. She was waiting at the door. A deputy was blocking her entry into the building. After a few moments, a voice came over his radio, and he allowed her in. She made her way toward me.

"Grace, what are you doing here?"

"It seems I have a knack for finding dead people."

"Oh no, Grace."

"I could ask you the same question, but I think I know the answer."

She smiled.

Neither one of us noticed Drew come up behind us.

"Emmie, ready for a trial run?"

With a broad smile on her face, she nodded at Drew.

Did they have a suspect? I wondered what she was going to be drawing. I followed them, hoping that by seeing her draw I could remember the rest of the dream she was in.

Drew led her to Vladimir. I tried to keep my distance, but I still wanted to be able to hear what he was saying. He seems to have been the last person to see Aleksandra alive, but he recalled seeing someone outside the theater as he was leaving to go back to his hotel room for a couple of hours before the performance.

"When I left, she was alive," he said in his thick Russian accent with broken English. "I go to her dressing room, and she put on her kimono and was to take off her pointe shoes. I gave her changes for tonight's performance. We talked for 10 minutes. Then I left. She was not leaving. She would rehearse and rehearse and rehearse. She was driven."

He shook his head.

"How is she dead?"

He started to cry again.

"I walked out of the theater. I saw a man standing outside. I left alone and walked back to the hotel. Is only a few blocks away."

I wasn't sure I believed his story. I couldn't believe Drew was taking him seriously, but I guess that was police work, following every lead, even if it wasn't plausible. The murder seemed personal to me. It wasn't some random person off the street. The killer knew the victim, and it was a vendetta. I wondered what was written on the mirror. If Drew knew what I was thinking, he'd probably laugh at me. For this murder case I was going to try and keep my mouth shut even though I knew I wouldn't be able to.

"Could you give a description to our sketch artist?"

"If I can remember," he said.

Drew turned to look at me. He raised an eyebrow and smiled. He walked toward me.

"What are you still doing here?"

I smiled.

"Eavesdropping?"

He smiled at me.

"What else was I supposed to do? I wasn't sure if I could leave."

"You gave your statement, didn't you?"

"Yes."

"Let me see your hands."

I was confused.

"Why?"

He raised an eyebrow at me without answering Dutifully, I held my hands out. He inspected them and then kissed the palm of one of them.

"No cuts or scrapes, which means you didn't have anything to do with that mess in there. You aren't a suspect unless you've learned how to write in Russian and didn't tell me about it," he grinned at me.

"I'm a quick learner but not that quick."

"Have you thought of something else?"

I looked at Emmie as she listened to Vladimir and drew someone according to his description. I couldn't hear what they were saying. They'd moved away from the crowd. I saw flashes of the dressing room in my mind. I saw people struggling, but nothing more. I wondered if this was me remembering parts of a dream or my brain projecting what it thought happened in that room.

I shook my head.

"No, nothing else. Except what's at my shop. A man came in earlier with an order of roses and sunflowers for our dead ballerina. He was just the messenger or so he said. I believe him. He was specific about getting the order here before 5:30, and the sender had typed a message in Russian for her so I have no idea what it said."

"Are you feeling well enough to drive back to your shop?"

He tilted his head at me when he said that.

"My knees aren't as shaky. I still feel like I'm going to throw up again, but I think I'll be fine to drive. It's not that far."

He had a skeptical look on his face.

"Do I need to find someone to drive you?

I tried to give him a weak smile. I didn't feel like smiling at all, but I had to get out of this place.

"Drew, I'll be all right."

He kissed me on the forehead and touched my cheek.

"I don't believe you, but you go ahead. I'll meet you there soon."

# 3

It didn't take long to make it back to my shop. I was glad I'd driven my personal vehicle instead of the delivery van with the business name and phone number on the side of it. When I left the theater, I saw a couple of the TV news vans parked out front. I didn't need anyone knowing who I was or following me. Fortunately, they didn't pay any attention to me.

I had only been back at the shop a few minutes when Beth arrived. She was wearing a short, sexy, strapless black cocktail dress with obscenely high stiletto heels.

"I'd break an ankle wearing those heels. What are you doing here?"

"Spill it," she said without batting an eyelash.

"What are you talking about?"

"Don't play innocent with me. We're doing flowers for the Russian ballerina, and I saw you get into your car and leave the theater."

"I didn't think you were going to go to the ballet performance."

"Well, I wasn't at first. That's a story for another day. Why was the performance cancelled? I checked the websites for the TV stations, and there's nothing there even though their vans are parked outside on Telfair Street, and the paper doesn't have any posts either. It looks like every cop in Augusta is there. So what do you know?"

"It's an open investigation."

Beth sighed.

"Stop talking like the police, Grace. Your husband is the homicide investigator, not you. He's not here, so you talk."

"I went to make a special flower delivery at the theater for Aleksandra."

I took a deep breath.

"When I got there, she was dead in the dressing room."

"Wow. The diva is dead?"

I nodded.

"I met her earlier today. She was nothing like what they said. I accidentally left my keys in her dressing room, and she was really nice. I didn't talk to her long. She seemed sad and lonely. She said all of it was a publicity stunt - the whole diva ballerina thing."

Beth chuckled nervously, and I looked at her.

"What?"

"If you aren't careful, you might get a nickname."

"What are you talking about?"

"The florist of death."

"Great. Thanks a lot."

"Well, two corpses near events you are doing flowers for is not good for building a business," she said.

"You're telling me, and it's not good for my mental health either."

I tried to laugh, but I just couldn't. All I could see were Aleksandra's eyes.

Beth cocked her head to the side and raised an eyebrow as she scrutinized my face.

"You do look a little pale, and you've lost some weight. I've noticed, but I haven't said anything."

I tried to break her gaze. I looked away and walked toward my office. She was starting to act like my mother.

"I'm waiting for Drew to show up. I might have some evidence for him."

I'd kept the note card the instructions were written on. I pulled it out and showed it to Beth who'd followed me.

"It's all in Russian so I have no idea what it means."

"Don't look at me. We were in French class together, remember?"

I laughed. I needed something to get my mind off what I'd seen. We were horrible in French class. I'm surprised we learned anything.

"So why were you at the ballet, and why didn't you get tickets for me? I thought I told you I wanted to see it."

"You did, and I'm sorry. I wasn't planning on going. You know I'm on several arts' boards. I went mainly to be their face. Besides, I wanted to spy on the ballerina. I'd heard she was amazing, and I wanted to see what all the buzz was about."

She smiled. As she was talking, Drew walked in.

"Are you okay, baby?"

He pulled me into his arms and held me for a minute.

"I don't know if I'm okay or not. I didn't think owning a floral shop would be so dangerous."

"Trying to make a joke is a good thing," he said softly.

I stepped back, and he turned to Beth.

"Hello, Beth. You're all gussied up tonight."

"Yes, I was supposed to see some Russian dancers, but I wasn't allowed to."

"The show must go on - just not tonight."

"Are either of you going to give me any details?"

Drew shook his head.

"Nope."

He smiled and winked at her much to her annoyance.

"Are you finished already?" I interrupted their small talk.

"No, I still need to go back, but I wanted to find out what was so important."

I handed him the note card and told him about the messenger.

"Maybe, there are some fingerprints or DNA or something on it. I don't know how all of that works."

"I'll see what I can find. You said he paid in cash?"

I nodded.

"Yeah, so no credit card receipt."

He looked at the card.

"Drew, I don't believe that artistic director. I think this killing was personal."

As I said that, an image flooded into my mind. I could see two people arguing and the argument escalating until someone pushed her into the mirror breaking the glass. Aleksandra tried to steady herself and placed her hands into the broken shards. The killer picked up a pair of pointe shoes and tied the ribbons around her neck. She reached for them, but she couldn't pull free. I didn't see anything else after that. I only saw them struggling.

"Grace, Grace."

"What? I'm sorry."

"What just happened?"

"A few days ago, I had a dream about Emmie, wearing a suit and sketching faces at a crime scene. And I couldn't remember anything else. Then it happened tonight. She was wearing the exact same suit as she was wearing in my dream. I just saw the murder flash before my eyes, but I can't remember if that was part of the dream I had or if it was just my imagination filling in the blanks with what I saw."

"It's okay, Grace. I don't believe Vladimir either. I don't believe any of the dancers we talked to. It could've been anyone in that theater."

"Why did you call Emmie out?"

"It's a trial run," said Emmie who'd walked in the work room door.

That would be good for her. I could see her doing this job well.

"Emmie, that is the ugliest suit I've ever seen. You were

wearing that exact same suit in my dream."

Emmie laughed.

"Yes, it is ugly, but it's functional. Do you remember anything else?"

"Sorry, Emmie. I don't."

"I don't mean to cut you off, babe, but do you have anything else for me?" Drew asked.

"No, that's it."

He turned to Beth.

"Beth, you know a lot of people in the arts community. On the slim chance that it wasn't a Russian in this ballet company, do you know of anyone who might not like having an outside group in town?"

Augusta has a thriving arts community and a legacy of influential artists, musicians, and authors. The godfather of soul, James Brown, made Augusta his home. Authors Frank Yerby and Berry Fleming had best-selling novels in the 1940s and had their works turned into films as did Louise Shivers in the 1980s. Pulitzer Prize winning poet Stephen Vincent Benet called Augusta home in the 19th century, and Oscar Wilde visited Augusta. Erskine Caldwell lived in nearby Wrens, Ga. and people in Augusta to this day still hate him for the way he portrayed Augustans in his books, Tobacco Road and God's Little Acre.

There are several ballet and dance companies, a symphony, and lots of community theater in the area as well as a multitude of talented visual artists, who turned the downtown part of the city into a creative hub. On the first Friday of the month, there are special arts events, and the Saturday market also had its share of artists and musicians. A couple of large arts festivals as well as indie movie film festivals are also part of Augusta's arts' scene. For a community of its size, Augusta has more than its fair share of talented artists. And Beth was on more boards than I could name.

Not only did we have homegrown performers and artists, the town attracted other shows as well. Traveling performers also came to town on a regular basis with a Broadway series at the theater where Aleksandra was killed, and top names in the music industry performed concerts at various venues in Richmond and Columbia Counties as well as across the Savannah River in Aiken, South Carolina.

Most artists and performers tended to be supportive of each other's endeavors, and I couldn't think of any time when they spoke out against each other or criticized anything at least publicly. With all the dance groups in town, there were four Nutcrackers in the span of a couple of weeks between Thanksgiving and Christmas one year, and no one seemed to complain. And there certainly weren't any dead bodies in any of the theaters.

Beth folded her arms.

"Well, I do know a few people who grumbled about this group taking money away from the other local dance groups. There's a woman who's on one of the boards I'm on. She's actually from Russia and has been pretty vocal about them coming."

"Really? How vocal?"

Beth shook her head. She looked like she'd wished she'd kept her mouth shut.

"She doesn't seem the violent type, Drew."

"No one ever does."

Beth shrugged her shoulders.

"Okay, then. I'd forgotten about it actually. This performance has been on the books for about nine months now."

"And?"

"The woman is named Irina Meadows. She used to be a dancer, but she married an American and settled down. Several months ago, she was angry that this specific ballet group was coming into town. She mentioned them at several luncheons I went to. I thought it was odd that she was so upset about this particular company coming into town. There have been other out of town dance groups here, but she's never said anything about them. She told me she sent a letter to the editor of the paper. She even wanted to get on one of the local radio talk shows to get people to boycott them. She seemed angry about all of it, but I haven't heard anything from her in a couple of months. Now, I'm wondering if there was some other reason she wasn't happy. I guess that does sound a little more incriminating than I thought."

"Keep talking, Beth, you're definitely incriminating her."

"I'm sorry. I think. Well, maybe not. Irina isn't the nicest of people. She's self-important, and I could see that she was probably a diva ballerina in her day."

She laughed nervously.

"Do you have a number or address for her?"

"I can get you one."

"Grace, it's going to be a late one. Are you going to be okay?"

"Stop asking me that, Drew. I'll be fine."

"You don't look fine, honey."

"She can stay with me tonight if she wants, Drew. The boys are with their dad even though it's not his night," Emmie interjected.

"I'm a big girl. I'll be fine. I'm going home and taking a hot shower and maybe I'll drink some tea or something."

Emmie and Drew both gave me looks that said they didn't believe me. I didn't want to be alone, but at 32, I was really too old to be afraid to stay by myself. And I wasn't giving them the pleasure of knowing they were right.

Drew leaned over to kiss me. He held me as he whispered in my ear.

"It's okay if you have to stay with Emmie. You aren't trained for this. We both know that."

He read my mind, but I let my pride get in the way.

"I appreciate you worrying about me, Drew. I really do, but I just need to breathe. I'll be okay."

He let me go and headed to the door.

"Beth, get me that info as soon as you can."

"I'm on it."

I walked into the back workroom and to the case where all of the orchids were stored. They'd paid for the orders in advance, but I wondered what I was going to do with all these flowers. There were quite a few of them.

As I was trying to figure out the course of action, my phone rang. It was someone from the theater management group. They wanted me to hold onto the flowers. The original performances were scheduled for Wednesday and Thursday. They were going to reschedule Wednesday's cancelled performance for Friday because there was nothing booked at the theater and someone with deep pockets apparently came through with the money needed to secure the site. So there would still be two nights of performances and the sponsor after-party. They wanted to have a memorial service at the theater on Friday morning. Each of the dancers would receive some of Aleksandra's flowers as part of the tribute. We decided that I could take her roses and orchids and create a small bouquet for each of the dancers to hold. There sure was a lot of money being thrown around for this performance. Tickets to the shows ranged from $75 to $150 each. Corporate tables were also available for a pretty penny. There was no way the ticket sales could recoup all the costs that I mentally tallied. It made me think there was something else going on. Maybe I was being paranoid, but things didn't add up.

I would still need to bring flowers to the theater on Thursday but not the rigorous order that I'd had before. I could make the bouquets in the morning. I was tired. It had been a long and trying day.

# 4

Once I got home, I stood in the shower and let the hot water beat down my back. I started to feel a little queasy again, and an irrational fear started rising from the pit of my stomach. I thought my knees might be shaking. I tried to focus my mind on something else - like figuring out how I could translate Russian into English. I couldn't get Aleksandra's face out of my mind. She was dead, but her gold-flecked, brown eyes had been wide open. I knew she couldn't see me, but at the same time, I felt as though she'd stared at me, pleading with me to help find her killer. I didn't want to let her down even though I knew my husband was the professional, not me. I would get past my fear and whatever these other feelings were to do whatever I could to help him.

I threw on a pair of shorts and a tank top and sat down at the computer. I'd made a copy of the card with the instructions on it for the flowers. I stared at the Russian characters. I opened my phone and scrolled through the photos, enlarging the one of the mirror. I compared the two side by side. They didn't say the same thing. I could tell that much anyway. I guess it would have been too convenient for our killer to be the same person as the one who sent the flowers. But then again, we didn't know who sent the flowers. The card didn't seem to be signed. Not knowing Russian, however, I couldn't be too sure.

I suppose the sender could've been a wealthy admirer with

no time to take care of the flowers. I was sure the delivery boy was just that - a delivery boy. Or maybe he was a crazy stalker, an admirer who fantasized that she was more than just a beautiful dancer, and he killed her because she didn't want to have anything to do with him. Now my imagination was running away with me. I'd watched too many late night movies.

I stared at the photos of the mirrors - the one with the red lipstick and then the smashed one. I zoomed in on that one. There looked like there was blood on the mirror, which supported my idea that Aleksandra was pushed into it at one point. The killer would have scratches or cuts from the struggle, I suppose, unless they were wearing gloves. And that would've been why Drew looked at my hands. I stopped scrolling through my photos. I couldn't look at the ones of the body. Why did I take those? What had I been thinking?

I decided to make myself a cup of tea and stood by the kitchen window for a few minutes lost in thought. Maybe I could get some answers from the dancers in the morning. There might be a chance to interact with them. But I couldn't ask them to translate what was written on the mirror or the card. One of them could've done it for all I knew. I didn't want to compromise Drew's investigation. I thought about trying to use a translation program on the Internet, but since I didn't have a keyboard with Russian letters, I didn't know how to make that happen.

A knock on the door brought me back to reality. I glanced at my kitchen clock. It was a little after 9. It seemed like it should be much later than that or even another day, but it wasn't.

I walked into the living room, and through the windows, I could see Emmie standing outside. She could see me through the front window and waved while grinning broadly. She held up a reusable grocery bag. I could only imagine what was in it.

"What are you doing here?" I asked as I opened the door. She breezed past me, ignoring my question. She looked around my house like she hadn't been here in a while. It didn't pass my mother's clean house inspection, but it was too late. Emmie was already inside and making her way toward the kitchen.

"Drew sent me a text. He was wondering where you were. He said he might be a little longer. Something about paperwork."

She made herself at home in my kitchen, pulling out two bowls from the cupboard and two spoons. She piled a couple of scoops of ice cream into the bowls.

"My husband sent you a text to check up on me? What am I like 14 or something?"

Emmie pushed a bowl of ice cream into my hands.

"Chocolate chip cookie dough ice cream does not solve everything, Emmie."

I put the bowl on the table. I love Emmie, but I wanted to be alone.

"No, it doesn't, but it makes me feel better. Just say 'thank you.'"

"That's because you don't gain any weight. Not all of us are blessed with your metabolism."

"Well, you've lost enough weight in the past month."

She handed me the bowl again. Not even ice cream could make me feel better. I put it down.

"You know I've always been trying to lose that last 10 pounds."

"I think you've lost more than that, and you look pale."

"I just haven't been hungry. Besides, compared to those dancers, I'm the size of a sumo wrestler."

Emmie laughed as she grabbed my bowl and walked out of the kitchen.

"At least you haven't lost your sense of humor."

"Sometimes, I'm not so sure. Besides, this has been really hard on my mental health. I'm the one who had to leave biology class and run to the bathroom to throw up, remember?"

"And that's the reason I'm here with ice cream therapy. You know this always helps."

She attempted to give me the bowl again.

"I can't eat ice cream."

"Then, this is worse than I thought," Emmie put her hand on her hip and stared at me. She walked over to my movie cabinet and started looking through my DVDs. "Vintage comedy always seems to help. Any preferences?"

I shook my head.

"I don't know if anything can help."

I walked over to the computer and picked the phone up off my desk. I looked at my phone and then at Emmie. I held it out to her.

"If you tell Drew what I'm about to show you, I will hunt you down and make your life miserable for all of eternity."

"Yes, ma'am," she said, mocking me with a salute.

I scrolled to the picture of Aleksandra's dead body and gave the phone to Emmie.

"This is the reason I don't want ice cream. I have images of two dead women stuck in my brain."

"Why is that on your phone? That really makes me not want ice cream now."

"I told you. That's why I've lost weight and don't want food. I have more pictures."

"I don't want to see that," she said, handing me the phone back.

"Just like I have these photos in my phone, I have photos in here," I pointed to my head. "I still see a beautiful young woman floating face up in the Savannah River. I can't erase her from there."

"That doesn't tell me why you have those photos. Drew is the professional, honey. You should remember that."

"Yes, I'm well aware of what Drew does. Everyone keeps reminding me of that, but you know good and darn well that if it hadn't been for you, Beth, and me, the last case might not have been solved the way it was. Even the FBI thanked us, and now they want you to work for them."

"I don't want to see you get involved."

"It's a little late for that, don't you think? I delivered flowers to a corpse today. Granted it's not the first time I've taken flowers to a dead person, but I wasn't discovering their murders when I delivered them."

"So what are you doing now?"

"Do you know anyone who can speak or read Russian?"

"No, I don't."

"Well, that's what I'm trying to do. There was a cryptic message written on the mirror, and there was a flower arrangement I delivered that also had a message written in Russian. I compared the two of them, and from what I saw, the messages weren't the same."

"So what else are you up to?"

Emmie looked at me.

"I'm thinking that I should go out and buy a trench coat and a fedora that I can wear at an angle just over my eye."

I pantomimed, angling the hat, and I winked at her.

"Maybe I could change my name to Nancy or Sam?"

Emmie shook her head at me.

"You're being ridiculous. Your sarcasm is noted."

"Who's being sarcastic?"

I raised my eyebrow, and Emmie didn't say anything.

"And why am I being ridiculous? I'm just trying to lighten the mood some instead of eating ice cream. I'm tired of crying so much lately," I took a deep breath. "Any information I can find to pass onto Drew can't hurt, can it? It just bothers me that I don't remember any more of the dream I had with you in that suit. Where did you get that ugly thing anyway? It's exactly like what I saw in the dream."

"Really? You didn't tell me what the suit looked like. I got it a few weeks ago before you had the dream. I'd been trying to decide whether or not to call them for an interview. It's so not me."

I gave Emmie a hug.

"I'm so happy for you. You're right. That suit is not you in the slightest, and it's the ugliest thing I've ever seen. And those shoes, oh my. Don't get me started on those."

She laughed.

"Yeah, I went for the ugliest ones I could find. I wasn't sure if ugly equaled professional or not."

"Those shoes are beyond awful."

I don't know why but the thought made me laugh.

"Well, they are comfortable."

She paused and then shot me that glance of hers she always gave me before suggesting something that would get both of us in trouble.

"Maybe we're supposed to be crime fighters together after all. We need superhero capes or something."

"You'd be my superhero right now if you spoke Russian."

"Habla espanol?"

I laughed. I walked over to the computer.

"I took French with Beth in high school, remember?"

"Who could forget? You almost burned the school down the day you tried to make crepes in class."

"Oh wow. I'd forgotten all about that. That wasn't Beth and me. We were slicing cheese and cutting up pieces of bread to make a beautiful presentation along with a bunch of grapes. That was Jenny Henderson who wasn't watching the crepes because she was drooling over that French foreign exchange student."

Emmie nodded. She had a faraway glance. I could tell she was drifting back in time.

"Yes, I remember that French guy. What was his name? He had the most beautiful blue eyes and that accent. None of us could understand a word he said, but we wanted to hear him talk," she smiled and shook her head.

"He could've cussed us out, but we wouldn't have cared."

While Emmie drifted off into another world, I sat down at the computer and tried to get back to what I'd attempted to do in the first place.

"So what are you looking for?" she asked.

"I was going to check Irina Meadows online to see if anything came up. I wonder what her name was before she got married."

"Her maiden name might be there if you pull up her social network profiles. A lot of people do that, you know."

Emmie sat on the chair next to me, eating her ice cream.

"I thought you weren't hungry after seeing my pictures."

"Don't judge me. Do you know how much this stuff costs? I bought the good kind of ice cream. None of that store brand, cheap stuff for my best friend who had a horror movie of a day, and you aren't even eating it."

I laughed.

"You're a great friend, Emmie. I appreciate you coming to cheer me up."

"That's what best friends do."

"Let's see what we can find."

It wasn't hard to find Irina Meadows online. She had profiles at several different sites. There were quite a few ramblings on her pages too. She was up in arms about the Russian dancers coming to town. I also found that letter to the editor of the local paper and the alternative weekly newspaper. She seemed to object to the ballet company's appearance because it would take away money that would benefit other arts groups. She also felt someplace like Atlanta or Charlotte would be a better fit. She even called on people to boycott the performance. How noble of her. But the skeptic in me thought there must be something else.

"Wow. What could have made her hate them so much?" Emmie asked as I read her the letter to the editor.

"I guess the real question is 'did she hate them enough to kill Aleksandra over it?'"

"Yes, you have a point."

Her profile was public so I started searching through her photos, and there were a couple of pictures of her and a woman who looked like a younger version of our dead ballerina.

"Well what do you know?" Emmie mused.

"That is definitely Aleksandra. It looks like they danced

together at one time so they did know each other."

They were smiling and wearing tutus after a performance in several photographs. Then there were pictures of Irina in a lift with a male dancer. I wondered who he was. She was beautiful in her tiaras and sequins. There were other pictures of her holding bouquets of roses. And her profile did have the Americanized version of her maiden name.

I typed in her name, but an Internet search in English didn't really come up with much. Putting Aleksandra and Irina's names into a search only led to a couple of news articles written in Russian. There was no option to translate them into English either.

"Yes, these photos are at least 15 years old. It looks like Irina was on her way out as Aleksandra was the up and coming star."

"That could be a reason to hate this group so much. Knowing you're being replaced by a younger model is never good for anyone's ego. How old was Aleksandra?"

"Our age. But I read that she started dancing almost as soon as she could walk and was climbing to the top of her profession when she was still a teenager. She was truly a dance prodigy. She took over with this company when she was only about 18."

We continued to scour the internet for photos or news articles, but I knew we were missing something.

"Maybe it wasn't Irina, maybe we should look at someone else in the company," said Emmie.

"True. I have a lot of suspicions about Natasha, a redheaded ballerina I met.

Emmie walked over to the table and reached into her giant oversized purse.

"Here's a copy of the program. I snagged one out of a box when I was in the theater earlier. It has everyone's name in it."

"That's good because I don't know what Natasha's last name is. She was really creepy. She asked me if Aleksandra had suffered. She seemed way too interested to me."

"Hmm. Sounds fishy to me too. Well, we have time. Let's see

if we can find anything on her."

I looked for the name, Natasha. Her biography was brief. She'd started dancing at a young age and received training at some prestigious Russian ballet schools. She'd performed leads in several ballet companies, but she was in the corps de ballet behind a famous name in this company. I'm sure that didn't do much for her ego. Was she a diva on the rise? It looked like she'd been in Aleksandra's shadow for several years.

"Do you think she was tired of hiding in the background? It looks like they were the same age, and it seems both had been with the company about the same amount of time," Emmie said.

"I guess that's possible."

"Natasha was in the wings while Aleksandra was in the spotlight. That doesn't do much for someone's ego."

We were so involved in the middle of our search and conversation that we didn't even hear Drew come in the back door. He always seemed to have impeccable timing to catch me in the middle of something I didn't want him to know about. He arrived to find us huddled around the computer.

"And what do we have here, Grace and Emmie?"

"Oh hi, Drew."

There was no hiding what we were doing.

"Hi to you, Grace. What's on the screen?"

"Just a few searches."

"I'll see you in the morning to help you work on the bouquets, sweetie," Emmie said as she headed to the door.

"Sure, go ahead and abandon me now. Some partner in crime you are."

She laughed.

"You're on your own."

"Thanks for the ice cream."

She laughed.

"You didn't eat yours, remember?"

I smiled.

"I'm sure it tasted fantastic."

Emmie waved and went out the front door.

"Find anything interesting?" Drew asked with his arms folded across his chest.

"The Internet is full of all kinds of interesting things."

"You know what I mean."

"You're looking at some of it."

"It looks like you've been busy."

"Well, Irina and Aleksandra knew each other, and it sounds like there was some bad blood there. And there's bad blood between Aleksandra and Natasha."

"And I intend on paying Irina a visit," said Drew. "I spoke with Natasha - sort of. All she kept saying was that she was innocent."

He knelt down in front of me and touched my face.

"But right now, I'm more concerned about you."

"I'm fine. Why wouldn't I be? "

"You can fool some people, but you can't fool me. I remember that day you bumped into that car near Augusta State, and that you were sick because of trying to dissect an animal in biology. You were still shaking from the ordeal when you had your accident that I was called to. If a dead frog does that to you, then what do the bodies of two dead women do?"

"It wasn't a frog; it was a cat."

He stood up and pulled me close to him.

"Just hold me, Drew, and everything will be fine."

"I know what you're going through. I still see the first dead body at my first traffic accident," he released me and looked into my eyes. "It was a young mother who wasn't wearing a seatbelt and went through the windshield into a tree. What was left of her wasn't a pretty picture. Her baby was fine in her car seat - like nothing had happened."

He shook his head.

"I understand now why you started drinking, Drew. I just want to wipe all of this out of my brain. It's like it's been tattooed there. I see it all the time."

He touched my cheek.

"I've been doing much better with that."

"I've noticed, and I'm glad."

"But the reason I did fall into that habit is still there. I see it every single day. It doesn't leave my mind, so I know exactly what you're talking about."

I nodded. He was talking about the deaths of his friends, Mark and Linda. It was a murder-suicide.

"Have you been able to talk about that?"

He tightened his jaw as he glared at me. I knew not to press it any further. It was still a hard subject for him, but he needed to talk about it. He still wouldn't talk to me about it. I didn't know what had happened just what I had read in the paper.

"You don't need to worry about me, but I'm still worried about you," he continued. "I want to take care of you."

I smiled.

"And that's why I love you."

He winked at me.

"Is that chocolate chip cookie dough ice cream on the table?"

"Yeah, Emmie brought it to cheer me up."

He walked over to the coffee table and picked up the bowl. That was the end of that other conversation.

"You aren't going to eat this?"

"It's melted now, but no, I'm fine."

He scooped up some of the cold soupy remains.

"Oh, she bought the good stuff. And you didn't eat this?"

I smiled. Drew stared at me.

"There's something wrong with this picture, babe. You're the ice cream lover, and you always talk more than I do. You're always full of questions."

I shrugged my shoulders. He sat down on the chair Emmie had occupied. It was close to the computer.

"Wanna sip?" he laughed as he held out of spoonful of the

sugary mix.

"I'll pass. I would still like to know what's going on with your case."

He sighed and put the bowl down on the edge of the desk.

"I don't have any information to pass on yet. We've gathered our evidence. We have a list of suspects. Emmie drew a couple of sketches. There are no security cameras in the dressing rooms or in the hallway. There's not a lot for us to go on right now except a whole lot of dancers who won't talk. We're looking for anybody who speaks Russian and has no ties to the ballet."

I nodded.

"You're the best, Drew. I know you'll find out who did this."

He reached out to touch my face.

"Don't take this the wrong way, but you look really tired. You've had dark circles under your eyes for a while now. And you're pale still. Let's get some sleep, and we can talk about this tomorrow. Okay?"

"I don't feel tired. I don't want to go to sleep. The last time I found a body I started having dreams about it. I really don't want to see the faces of two dead women in my sleep. I already see them when I'm awake."

Drew stood up and reached for my hands. He coaxed me out of the chair and pulled me into his arms.

"I'll protect you," he said.

I smiled and shook my head. I looked at him. His eyes seemed to bore into me. I could see how concerned he was. He ran his thumb across my cheekbone.

"I don't think you can save me from me."

"Let me at least try, babe. You saved me from me."

He gave me a quick kiss.

"Come on and get some sleep."

# 5

Drew cradled me in his arms all night. I think I slept. I wasn't really sure. I kept having dreams all night. Why I started having them now instead of before is beyond me. I really would've like to have been warned about the dead body, but it just proved I couldn't control what happened when I slept. One of the dreams stood out. It was of Aleksandra. She was still alive. In one scene, I saw her dancing. She was wearing a white tutu with shimmering silver sequins on it; a rhinestone-studded tiara sat upon her head. I'd never seen anything glitter as much as those costume pieces. Aleksandra was stunning as she spun around and around. At the end, she bowed to the standing crowd, and a man came out on stage bearing an armload of her lavender roses with the rhinestones glued to them. I saw his face. He had jet black hair, high cheek bones, a pronounced nose, and cleft chin. He wore a tuxedo and kissed her on both cheeks. He paused to gaze into her eyes and briefly touch her cheek before he left the stage. She radiated as she looked at him. She mouthed something to him. Despite the language barrier, no translation was needed. That was the look of two people who were passionately in love with one another.

I woke up to the smell of coffee and bacon. I tried to sit up. I felt drained and exhausted. A night filled with dreams often did that to me. But I was also trying to run through the seemingly endless sea of faces at the theater the night before. I kept thinking of the man with Aleksandra. Surely I would've noticed him because of those distinct facial features, but I couldn't recall seeing him.

I looked at the clock; 6:30 came early. It was late for Drew though. I dragged myself into the kitchen to find him at the table, drinking a cup of coffee.

"Good morning, sunshine," he smiled.

"You're chipper this morning."

"I've already had two cups of coffee. You really should try it sometimes."

"Burnt water. No thanks. I'll have some of that bacon though, and I think I'll have some sweet tea. Sugar and caffeine. It's just cold and has a good flavor," I said as I made my way to the refrigerator.

He laughed.

I trudged back to the table. I could've slept another hour. Why was I awake?

"Not that I don't want to have breakfast with you, but aren't you running a little late today?"

"I love you too, Grace. I've been up reviewing some things," he said. "How are you feeling today? You didn't sleep well last night."

"Oh? I didn't?"

I sat down across from him. Maybe that's the reason I was so tired.

"You tossed and turned a lot."

"Oh, I thought you held me most of the night."

"I tried, but you beat me away."

"Really? That's strange."

"I think I might have a bruise or two."

He laughed as he bent over to roll up his pants leg.

"That's okay. I believe you. I just thought I slept better than I had in a while."

He shook his head as he looked at me. I thought he wanted to say something, but he didn't.

"Why do you keep staring at me? And what was up with sending Emmie over last night? You do know I'm a grown woman."

"Your snarky comment is noted. Yes, I'm well aware of how

much of a grown woman you are," Drew said with a sly grin and a wink. "Seriously, though, I just asked Emmie to check on you. I didn't expect her to come over, but Emmie and Beth are right about you. Since seeing the body in the Savannah River last month, you haven't been the same. And when I saw your face at the theater yesterday..."

His voice trailed off.

"I'm fine."

That came out harsher than I expected. I didn't mean to snap at him.

"No, you're not. Don't keep saying that."

I took in a deep breath and looked away. I just wanted people to stop asking me so many questions and to stop treating me like I was a kid. He seemed to want to say something to me. I'd known him long enough to be able to tell when he was thinking carefully about how to word something before he said it to me. This was one of those times.

"What was going on with you last night?" he asked.

"I don't know what you mean."

I hadn't said much about dreams lately. If I was restless, it could've been related to that. He hadn't been shutting me out about them since they did prove to be true concerning his last murder case, but I was still hesitant to say the "d" word around him. He tilted his head to the side and smiled.

"Don't play innocent with me. What were you dreaming about?"

It surprised me that he said that. I paused for a moment before I said anything. I wanted to choose my words carefully.

"I dream most nights."

He sighed.

"And?"

"I think I dreamed all night, but I only remember one of them. I saw our victim, but she was alive."

Drew laughed so I stopped.

"What did I say?"

"'Our' victim?" he asked with a raised eyebrow. "Are you hanging up your shears and ribbons for a life in law enforcement?"

I ignored his comment.

"Anyway, Aleksandra looked so happy and in love. I saw her with a man. I could see his face so clearly. I wonder if he has anything to do with her death."

He nodded, and there was an awkward silence for a few moments. He wasn't going to take my dream seriously so I figured I should just talk about something else.

"You've changed since your first murder case."

"For the better?" he asked then took a sip of his coffee.

"Definitely. You aren't drinking nearly as much. You aren't nearly as angry. "

I did like the changes I'd been seeing in him, but there was still a part of me that thought he might be hiding something. No one was this happy at 6:30 in the morning, and Drew had never been a morning person. I hadn't seen him drinking like he had been, but there was still a bottle of liquor in the living room. To be honest, I hadn't been paying much attention to it. He was right. I had withdrawn from so many things. I guess I'd just keep watching his actions to see if he'd really changed for good. I knew it was awful to be suspicious of him, but I couldn't help thinking that he was still dealing with his anger and frustration in the wrong way. I was pretty sure he wouldn't turn to drugs because it could cost him his job. And because of his job, he knew how to wear the right mask to keep people guessing - even me.

"Grace, you are the most important part of my life, and you're a part I'm not ever going to lose. I came so close to losing you twice in April. I'm not about to let that happen again. I'm not perfect. I never claimed to be."

He'd stopped eating and reached out to touch my hand.

"I never asked for perfect."

"I know, and that's what I love about you. You take me with

my flaws and all."

"I love you too, Drew."

"And I took your advice. You know me better than anyone else. A lot of things woke me up to the realization that I could lose you - the day you stormed out of the house after you confronted me with my drinking and the crazy way my last case almost ended. I didn't know that the way I was trying to cope was actually pushing you away."

I didn't respond. I just let him talk.

"It's amazing what a couple of hours a week in a fishing boat on the lake talking to the Man upstairs can do for you. I've been working out more, getting rid of my frustrations that way. You know what they say about endorphins. I've always known it was true. Plus, I've been talking to Pastor B, and I'm in counseling. You know all of that."

"I do."

"Sometimes, we just forget what's important and something has to happen to jolt us back to reality."

I nodded.

"You should try it," he said.

"Which part? Sitting in a fishing boat on the lake a couple of hours a week or working out?"

He laughed.

"No, I can't see you baiting a hook, but the talking to the Man upstairs or to anyone for that matter would help. You got angry at me for abandoning my faith, but I could say the same thing about you right now."

I didn't know how to respond to that comment so I blurted out the first thing that came to mind.

"But you were right when you said people don't understand."

"Yes and no. I was wrong too. Sometimes people don't need to understand exactly what you are going through. Sometimes, you just need someone to listen to your fears and anger without telling you you're wrong to feel the way you do. Where the anger comes from doesn't matter; it's how you deal with it. Everyone gets angry, but not everyone turns to alcohol to drown their pain. You can talk to me, you know."

I nodded.

"And you could tell me about Mark and Linda, Drew."

I saw a slight pulse in his temple. I should've known from last night not to broach that subject, but he needed to face it. Maybe he would do it in his own timing.

"Emmie said you don't talk as much to her anymore either."

He brushed off my previous comment. I knew he would.

"You're getting awfully chummy with Emmie, Drew."

Drew narrowed his eyes at me.

"I can't believe you just said that, Grace."

"I'm not saying anything, but you seem to talk to her more than you talk to me."

Drew wasn't the only one who couldn't believe what I'd just said. I was stunned that I just implied something was going on with them. I was definitely on edge. What was wrong with me? I wasn't someone who liked confrontation, but here I was pushing his buttons on Mark and Linda and then that off-the-wall comment about Emmie. I knew there wasn't anything going on between the two of them. She'd actually gone on a few dates recently with Butch, a deputy Drew worked with. I guess I wanted to get past the superficial stuff he was showing me. Maybe I thought by pressing him, I could get him to talk to me about what was still lingering below the surface. Or it could've been that I didn't want him to see me like this - unsure and afraid. That was stupid. I knew Drew loved me. I'd never hidden my feelings from him for long. Plus he was right about my faith. It had been shaken.

"I'm not fighting with you this early in the morning," he said. He narrowed his eyes at me slightly, and I could see his jaw clenching.

This wasn't how I wanted to start my day.

"I don't want to fight with you, either, but I just don't feel you are facing the things that are still bothering you."

He took a deep breath.

"Emmie has called me to talk about you. She's worried about you. She says you're distant at the shop. It's like you're not there. You're distracted. You forget things. You don't eat. You don't realize your friends are even there. That's not like you, and that's one of the reasons Emmie's hesitant to take the jobs she's been offered. She wants to be there for you. She's afraid to leave you."

I had no idea, but he was changing the subject again. We weren't going to touch on what was really bothering him anytime soon. I guess I just needed to face that fact. He'd talk to me when he was ready and not before then. And maybe I didn't want to talk about what was bothering me either.

"I'm sorry, Drew. I didn't mean that."

"Grace, where are you?"

"I'm not sure, but I wish you'd quit asking me. It's not helping."

He paused and there was that look from earlier. He looked away. I thought he wanted to say something, but he just stared at the wall for a few moments before turning back to me.

"You're probably not going to like this," he said. He'd dropped his tone. That was the tone I usually heard when he wasn't happy about something I'd done.

"That's a heck of a way to start a sentence."

"Well, it's true. Look, I don't do this often, but I've made an executive decision. We - you and I - are going to the beach in a couple of weeks. Both of us need some time away especially you. I know you love the beach and going there clears your head. And what happened yesterday made me realize that I can't put this off any longer. I've talked to Beth - "

I didn't want him to talk to Beth. I shook my head and started to stand up. Drew interrupted before I could get the words out.

"I told you you weren't going to like it, but I don't care. I know you don't like letting her know your problems, which I don't really understand. She's your friend, isn't she? And it's not like she's blind. Do you know Beth? The woman should be a detective. And if you think she doesn't know what's going on with you, then you've got another thing coming. She told me things about you that I didn't even know."

"Like what?"

What he said about Beth was the truth . She knew what was going on around town, but as I found out during Drew's last case she did keep some secrets secret until she thought they might be of use. She didn't tell what she knew just to make conversation. She liked being the keeper of secrets, I think.

"She's come to me with the whole baby thing and the dead body and the pressures of the shop," Drew continued. "She's agreed to let us use their house at Edisto for a week or longer if necessary. And she's willing to take on managing the shop while you're gone. You know she'll do a great job."

I knew he was right. I guess deep down I was jealous of Beth, but she really was a friend. She always came through for me. Maybe I did need to get away, and Edisto was the perfect place to just forget about things for a while. I loved Edisto. It was a beautiful natural beach in South Carolina as far from commercial as was possible in the 21st century. There were only a handful of shops and a couple of restaurants, but it had beautiful vistas and clean fresh air. Sometimes, my cell phone didn't even work when I went there. Beth's beach house was the perfect getaway. It had wrap-around screened porches and was so peaceful. And that was exactly what I needed. The sound of the ocean crashing on the beach was healing. We both needed healing.

"After dead body number two, I think you're right. I can't keep going like this."

"So am I forgiven?"

"Of course you are, Drew. I don't usually stay mad at you for long."

"And back to your dream, when you see Emmie today, why don't you ask her to sketch the mystery man for us?"

I was shocked and all I could do was nod my head. Now I knew he was hiding something or overcompensating. He'd been so adamant about not hearing my dreams, and now he was encouraging me in them? It didn't make sense. Or maybe all of this murder was making me ask too many unnecessary questions.

"Did you find out anything else last night?"

"Only that I wished I knew Russian because those dancers were talking to each other, but not to me. I've got to go. I have a couple of things to do. I'll see you later."

He gave me a quick kiss and headed toward the door. All the talk of the beach and my dream had diverted me from the questions I wanted to ask him about the case. Good move, Drew. I couldn't figure him out. Sometimes, he seemed to want me to help him especially when I'd been at two crime scenes and found two bodies. And he did show a little interest in my dream by asking me to get Emmie to sketch the guy I saw. Then he'd do an about face and not want me to know anything that was going on.

"I don't want anything to happen to you," I could imagine him saying.

Too bad, Drew, I'm helping you anyway. It's too late for me not to help.

Now that I had an image in my mind of a possible love interest for our dead ballerina I thought I'd take a few more minutes to do a search on the Internet. I wasn't looking for him before. If she'd been a singer or a movie star, it would have been easy to find out more information, but sadly she wasn't really paparazzi fodder, and her name hadn't been combined with a man's like the media had done with so many other famous couples.

I searched for members of the Russian ballet theater. Nothing. I guess Drew was right. I wasn't an investigator and should probably leave things to the professionals. I could get back to it once I got into the shop. I felt like I needed to take a walk or something to clear my mind. I grabbed a bottle of water and left the house.

# 6

I decided to head to Riverwalk. It was a beautiful May morning, and I knew that dead bodies there were the exception rather than the rule. I always thought of it as a safe place especially during the day. I didn't think I'd stumble into any danger, but I decided I needed another view of the river not the one closest to the amphitheater where I'd found the last body. I needed to get the image of a dead woman floating face up out of my mind so I headed down river. It was the perfect morning for wandering aimlessly or just sitting and staring.

The Savannah River was peaceful as it ambled on its way. It wasn't a quick river at this point in its course. It was slow and steady. I stood near the green railing and peered into the water. There were several ducks gliding on the surface, and I could see the head of a turtle as it swam toward the bank. Mourning doves cooed nearby and a bright red cardinal lighted on the limb of one of the trees overshadowing the river. The sound of a train passing over the Fifth Street trellis and its whistle briefly broke through my reverie and jolted me back to reality. I glanced in that direction. The spot where the tracks crossed the Savannah from South Carolina into Georgia was a popular place with photographers for wedding, engagement, and prom photos. And it wasn't hard to see why - especially on a day like today when the clouds were white wisps painted on the cerulean sky.

I thought back over the weeks that had passed since the last time I'd come to the river. I shook off the nervous dread that seemed to rise under my emotions. There were no dead bodies here today. There were very few people at all.

I thought about what Drew had said at breakfast. Things with Drew had gotten better over the past few weeks. True to his word, he started counseling the week after his first murder case had wrapped up. He seemed calmer, gentler. He was returning to the man I married. He brought me small presents after work. Nothing extravagant, just small gestures - smoothies, tea, cupcakes, the occasional wildflower that he'd picked off the side of the road, books, and things he knew I liked.

But there was part of me that wondered how long it was going to last, and I wasn't sure why I felt this way. It wasn't like he'd been an alcoholic all of our marriage. I knew his drinking had been a coping mechanism for the deaths of Mark and Linda. Part of me wondered if he was going to counseling just to placate me not because he was interested in fixing his drinking problem. I knew he held onto a lot of anger concerning Mark and Linda. He had punished himself as though he had caused their deaths. It wasn't true. He tried to save them, but he couldn't. There was nothing he could've done. So while some of the outward appearances had changed, I knew what was at the heart of his pain wasn't being dealt with at all. If it wasn't dealt with, it would only lead to a major relapse in the future. And I wondered why I kept thinking he was going to fall back in that habit. It was a stupid thought.

There was no talk of children either. I'd asked for a moratorium on the subject, but I was surprised at how quickly it became taboo, even my mother didn't mention it. Well, almost everyone stopped talking about it. Drew's mother wouldn't let up on it. At the party she had for Drew's promotion, she said rather loudly on several occasions how she wanted the next party she attended to be a baby shower for our baby. I almost broke down in tears and had to leave. I stayed for Drew's sake, but it was all I could do. My mother shielded me from some of it with her wonderful sense of humor and charm. She deflected some of the comments from me.

Drew said something about it to his mother after the party. She got upset or embarrassed or something and had kept her distance since. One more relationship I was responsible for ruining, I suppose. I still hadn't gone to see Dana Andrews, my longtime friend, and her beautiful new bundle of joy. And I felt incredibly guilty about it. I did send her a card with a brief note apologizing. She sent a note back on her monogrammed note cards that she thought she knew what was going on and would be there to talk whenever I could. She thanked me for the flower arrangements and told me she was impressed with my talents. She said the flowers made her days. I'd smiled because it was Emmie and Beth's talents she was reaping the benefit of, not mine. It was a start. I still felt like a horrible person because of all of it. I should've been a more supportive friend, but now that we'd drifted apart, I wasn't sure how to fix the problems or if I even had the energy to try. And with the way her husband had railed at me when he came into my shop that day, I wasn't sure that was a bridge that would be crossed back over any time soon.

While I'd wanted all the talk of babies to stop, there was a part of me that felt something died when it did. Maybe it was the glimmer of hope that had already been fading away. My brother would be moving back over the summer with his brood and the new one on the way. They'd found a house about 10 minutes from my mother's. I knew that would make her happy to have all the grandchildren around. I'm not sure why not having children made me feel like such a failure. This was the 21st century after all. I knew my worth wasn't equated with my ability to produce children, but I still felt empty. Being around women with babies magnified that feeling in me. I wasn't sure how I could avoid seeing my mother and brother. I secretly hoped his orders might get changed, and he'd be sent someplace like Washington state or Arizona. I didn't want to accept what kept staring me in the face.

Drew was right. I hadn't been praying or "talking to the Man upstairs" as he liked to say much lately, and I hadn't been taking the time to enjoy life. I didn't know what to say or how to say it. And despite the fact that I handled roses almost every day, I didn't stop to smell them or admire their beauty any more.

The wind blew my hair into my face. I turned away from the water to push the strands out of my eyes. I became vaguely aware of a couple of mothers power-walking through the area with babies in their aerodynamic strollers. There were a few joggers passing through as well. It was a beautiful day to walk, but it was already starting to get balmy outside. Summer time was in the air even if the calendar didn't reflect it. I could feel the sweat on my neck. I took a deep breath and looked at my phone. I was going to be late getting the shop open if I didn't get a move on. I had too much to do, but I was glad I'd taken the time to stop for a minute. Downtown Augusta was a beautiful place. I needed to do this more often.

As I started to walk back to my car, I heard a voice behind me.

"Wait."

I turned around. It was Natasha, and she was alone.

"Yes?"

"You are the one from the theater," she said in a thick Russian accent.

"Yes."

"You found Aleksandra - dead?"

"Yes, how did you find me?"

"I came for a walk. We are at the hotel on the river. I saw you sitting there."

I nodded, wondering what she wanted. I could tell she was struggling for her words. English was not her native language; her sentences were stilted and labored.

"Do not believe all people will tell you," she said in her broken English.

"Okay? Why are you telling me this?"

"You are involved with the police detective, no?"

I nodded.

"Yes, he's my husband."

"Things are not as they seem," she said. "People are not as they pretend to be."

"I still don't know why you're telling me this."

"Because people will tell you things about me. I'm Aleksandra's - how do you say?" she paused and looked off into the distance. She wrinkled her mouth and snapped her fingers while she struggled for the right word. "Understudy. Yes, that's the word. I take her place if she cannot perform."

I nodded.

"Makes me look guilty, no?"

"I see."

"No, you do not see. I work hard. I dance. I have wanted to dance all my life. I started when I was 3. My mother sacrificed for me to dance. Aleksandra was not my friend, but I did not kill her. Yes, I wanted to take her place, but I am good enough. I work hard enough. I knew someone would see me. Now that she is gone, I dance in her place. But I did not kill her."

"Is that the only reason people would think you wanted her dead?"

She shook her head.

"Aleksandra and I fight. We fight much. We had different vision of dance. I am more artistic and have more technique than she did. She had great talent. She demanded more rehearsals so we could be perfect. She was not lazy, but she had to practice more to be better. Other dancers - they are lazy. I believe in hard work too. I am like Aleksandra, but I do not have to work as hard as she did."

I nodded.

"Those fights. People will tell. They will tell your husband."

I didn't know if I believed her or not. Was I supposed to tell Drew this?

"Why did you want to know if she suffered?"

"Do you know what it is like to be in pointe shoes for hours upon hours a day?"

I shook my head. My ballet training didn't take me that far.

"Is torture. My feet and toes bleed. She made us rehearse extra. She tortured us."

I nodded. Beth actually made it through to pointe in ballet. I remember her telling us of her toes bleeding. I nodded, but I thought maybe she'd clear something up for me.

"I met her - Aleksandra. She seemed to be very different from the picture people painted. She was nice ."

"Yes. Things are not always as they seem. She might be nice to you, but she was not nice to me. And I am glad I do not have to dance with her anymore. I am glad she is gone."

"I wish I could've seen her dance."

"She was grand and beautiful when she danced, but I am better. I did not kill her."

She stared at me.

"I will see you at the theater, no?" she asked. This time she smiled.

"Yes, I'll be there."

"Good."

She nodded and walked down Riverwalk. I watched her and tried to figure out what had just happened. Was I supposed to give her brownie points or something? Did she want me to tell Drew all of this? I couldn't shake any of this as I headed back to the shop, where Jazzy was waiting for me. She didn't have a key, and she was early as always. Actually, I was running a little late, but still, Jazzy arrived about 20 minutes before she was scheduled. Beth had helped her find a deal on a good used car, and we were all trying to help her get on her feet since getting her out of the sex industry. And she was thankful to have a chance at a new life; something she let us know on a regular basis.

She had become the highlight of my days. The shop was dreary when she wasn't around. She had such a bubbly personality. None of what she had gone through seemed to affect her, but Beth did have her talking with a counselor. It was refreshing to be around her. And I was probably wrong about no one being happy at the crack of dawn. Jazzy was a morning person, an afternoon person, and an evening person all in one.

"Miss Grace," she surprised me by giving me a big hug after I opened the door.

I was startled by the hug, and it must've shown in my face.

"You just looked like you needed a hug."

"Thanks. Yesterday was rough."

"I heard. So what do we have today? You sent me a text about memorial bouquets and baby arrangements. I love flowers. And I love this job. Thank you."

Jazzy liked to talk, and she did go from subject to subject with ease. But this morning something was off, and I wasn't sure what it was.

"Jazzy, is everything okay?"

She nodded her head "yes," then started shaking her head "no." I think I even saw a bit of a frown.

"What's wrong?"

"You know summer semester starts next week. I haven't been to school in so long. All those tests I had to take to get in were hard. I'm nervous about all of it."

"You'll do great."

"I know I've told you this, but I can be here when I'm not in school. I'll be helping with Miss Beth's babies too, and Miss Emmie said that she'll let me babysit."

"When are you going to study, Jazzy?"

"Oh, there's lots of time. I don't sleep much - so after midnight probably. I always wanted to go to college. I know I can make a difference. I used to be smart."

"You still are smart. You proved it by your scores on all those tests."

Jazzy had decided she wanted to get a two-year degree in medical assisting, and if she liked that, she hoped to become a nurse or even a physician assistant one day. She wanted to take it slowly especially since she'd been out of school for a while. She was going to take a few remedial courses over the summer to get back into the swing of school. She wasn't sure she was ready to tackle some of the classes needed to get into nursing school yet. Jazzy underestimated herself. She was more than smart. She'd scored high on the placement tests required to get into school. And according to the school, she didn't need to take the remedial courses. She breezed through the general equivalency test to get her high school diploma.

"I hope so."

I put my hand on her shoulder.

"You'll do great, and Beth knows a lot of people who can tutor you if you run into problems. But she doesn't think you'll need her help."

"I know. She told me too. I still can't believe all y'all want to help someone like me."

"What does that even mean? Someone like you? You are funny, beautiful, talented, and intelligent. Of course, we want to help someone like you."

She shook her head.

"Y'all know what I mean."

"No, I have no idea what you're talking about, and I have too much work to do to argue with you."

While we didn't want to ignore her past, we didn't want to dwell on it either. We didn't judge her by where she came from, and we went to great lengths to let her know that.,

She smiled at me as I checked the computer and voice mail for new orders. I had a few that needed to go to the theater today. I thought it was odd considering the private nature of the memorial service or whatever you wanted to call it. I looked through the list of orders. Several arts groups had placed orders for orchids - not the rare ones Aleksandra had wanted, but orchids nonetheless. Beth served on several boards. I could only imagine she had something to do with this. It was a nice gesture on their parts.

"I'm going to be taking the orchids we originally ordered for Aleksandra and making them into small bouquets for the dancers to hold during a memorial service for her tomorrow. That's what they told me to do with them. We'll also add some of the lavender roses. I've got a list with all of the names of the members of the company as well as the staff that is traveling with them. The men will receive a single rose to simplify things."

"Yes, ma'am. I'm on it."

I walked into the work room and pulled a few of the orchids and roses out, fashioning them into a small bouquet for Jazzy to duplicate. I added black and lavender satin ribbons and white tulle to the mix. The admirer had specified white tulle so I assumed there was something behind it that meant something to Aleksandra. We also took single blooms for the dancers to wear tucked into their costumes in her memory.

"That's really pretty, Miss Grace. You go have some tea, and I'll handle this. Don't you worry about a thing."

"Are you sure you don't want a hand in finishing them? I think we need to do about 25 when you count the dancers and others we have to make them for."

"I've got this," she beamed.

I smiled. I knew she did. I wasn't so sure medical assisting was the thing for her. I didn't really want to talk her out of it, but she had an eye for color and a style all her own. I remembered how she told me about wanting to decorate things when we were stuck in the warehouse together on the day we met. I'd mentioned the flower shop at one point in the conversation, and I could hear the excitement in her voice. She'd been in some of my meetings with brides about their floral arrangements. She came up with some ideas that blew them away.

She said I should have tea. A nice tall, glass of sweet tea definitely would've hit the spot, but I wasn't sure I had time for that. So many things were going through my head. I was more interested in what Drew was doing than ordering flowers or arranging them. I thought about returning to an internet search, but I wasn't sure what good that would do. I didn't know the man's name so it would be hard to search images on the computer. And I reminded myself that I wasn't the detective on this so I went into my office to do exciting paperwork. I resisted the urge to call Emmie. She wasn't supposed to come in today; she was going to help me at the memorial service. I did send her a text though telling her briefly about my dream and Drew's suggestion of having her sketch the man.

She didn't respond with a text, but in less than 20 minutes, a white paper cup appeared on my desk. As I looked up, I saw Emmie standing there with a big grin.

"Sweet tea. Are you a mind reader today?" I asked as I picked up the cup.

"Not a mind reader. But you function better when you have sugar and caffeine in your system ."

"Do you have a sketchbook?"

"Of course. That's the reason I'm here. Fire away."

She pulled her sketchbook out of her bag and sat in the chair in front of my desk.

I started describing him to her, but I paused as she started shaking her head and staring at the image that was taking shape.

"What?"

"Just keep giving me your description, sweetie," she said without looking up.

So I continued. He had such pronounced features. When I was finished, she handed me her sketchpad. Emmie captured him perfectly. I shook my head. It was as though she photographed the image I saw in my dream.

"You're amazing, Emmie. That's the man I saw."

She nodded, but she had a shocked look on her face.

"What's wrong?"

"Are you sure that he was only in your dream?"

"Yes, I'm positive. Why?"

She pulled out her phone and pulled up something before

she handed it to me. I stared at the photo. It was a sketch that looked almost exactly like the one she'd just drawn. I glanced at her sketchpad and then I glanced at her phone.

"What's this?"

"That's the man that Vladimir said he saw standing outside the theater."

"You aren't serious?"

She nodded.

"There was no one there when I arrived, Emmie. I swear."

"I believe you, Grace."

She paused for a minute and looked at both of the drawings again before she looked up at me and winked.

"He's quite a looker," she said.

"Yes, he's handsome. I wonder who he is. I'm positive I didn't see him. There was no one there."

"Grace, you don't have to convince me. I know that what you see in your dreams is real."

"He's very tall. He's at least six-foot four maybe taller. He seems like he'd stand out in a crowd."

"I bet they were stunning together. She had such a beautiful face from the photos I've seen."

"She had a gorgeous complexion. It was spotless."

"So now what?"

"I'm not sure. I don't know how to search the internet for a nameless face. We need some of that facial recognition software I'm always seeing on those crime shows on TV."

Emmie laughed.

"I gave the sketch to Drew, but he didn't say what they might do with it. I don't think he really believed Vladimir's story. You know, I bet we know someone who has access to that fancy stuff."

"I don't know if the sheriff's department has that. Drew and I never talk about stuff like that."

"I'm not talking about Drew, sweetie. I'm talking about our friend at the FBI. You just helped him get a break in a huge case."

"I couldn't do that. Besides, I don't know how to get in touch with him."

Emmie reached into her jeans' pocket and pulled out a business card.

"Maybe you couldn't, but I could. He's the one who told me about the job, and he called me a couple of days ago. This could help the both of us."

She grinned at me.

"All right, then you call him, but remember, I didn't put you up to this because I know it will get back to Drew. And I don't want him upset with me."

I could tell she didn't need any convincing. She didn't get through to Agent Monroe, but she left him a message and sent him a text with photos of both sketches.

"There, it's done. Besides, this guy could be on some international data base or something. He may not even be an American. I doubt he is."

"True."

"Hey, I have an idea. You need some sun, and I'm starving. You have this vampire paleness going on that's not attractive at all. Let's talk and walk down Broad Street. I'm dying for a burrito."

"Thanks for the vote of confidence, Emmie."

"You burn every summer so let's just get you a little sun first okay?"

"But I've got things to do here."

"I've got it all under control," a Cajun-twanged voice called out.

"Wow, she's got great ears," said Emmie.

"I heard that."

Jazzy popped her head into the office. She had a broad grin on her face.

"You gals go on. I've got it under control, and if anything comes up, I have the two of you on speed dial plus your husband if things get real bad."

"I sincerely hope you don't have to call my husband."

"You ain't lying, but if I need the cops, I got the best on speed dial."

I laughed.

"Do you want anything, Jazzy?" Emmie asked.

"When you can get some jambalaya like my grand mama used to make, then you can bring me something."

"Sorry, there's no jambalaya where we're going, just really good burritos and nachos."

"I'll pass," she said.

"I'm driving," said Emmie.

It didn't take long to get to Broad Street, but it did take a few minutes to find a parking space. Broad Street lived up to its name. In the heart of Augusta's downtown district with its blend of shops, restaurants, few tall business buildings and apartment lofts, the street was four lanes wide with parallel parking on each side and a center strip of parking. In between the sections of parking , there were sitting areas with benches and fountains interspersed with azaleas, other plants and a couple of monuments. Emmie found a space in one of the center parking pits. I don't know the proper word for them. We'd just always called them the parking pits because they were lower than street level. We parked in the pit near the James Brown statue across from the Augusta Common, and Emmie insisted on taking a selfie near the Godfather of Soul's smiling bronze likeness. The singer, who called Augusta home for most of his life, was wearing his signature cape and holding a microphone on a stand. The statue was a popular photo spot.

"I thought you were starving, Emmie."

"I am, but I missed the big James Brown birthday bash a few weeks ago, and I need to pay my respects to the Godfather."

She wrestled with her phone for a few seconds trying to get both her and the statue in the photo. She wrinkled her nose.

"I'm not getting enough of the statue in the picture. Here, you take it for me. I want several," she said as she handed me her phone.

As she did her silly Emmie poses and I snapped a heard two female voices, carrying through the atmosphere. know why they caught my attention. I couldn't make out w[illegible]y were saying. Then I realized the reason. It wasn't that their words were garbled; they were speaking Russian. I caught them out of the corner of my eye. They were walking past the statue and heading down Broad Street, and I recognized them. One was Anna, the ballet mistress for the Russian Ballet, and the other was Irina Meadows. I knew her from her social media photos. In her early 50s, Irina Meadows was tall and slender. She still looked as though she could glide across the stage. Her platinum blonde hair was sleeked back into a tight bun. Emmie had left the statue and was by my side. She grabbed my arm and linked her elbow with mine.

"Keep your head down," she said. "Let's walk."

We walked briskly but tried to keep our distance behind the two women. They were engrossed in a conversation and weren't paying any attention to us. They stopped at the cafe near The Book Tavern, my favorite indie book shop, so we ducked inside. We tried not to draw attention to ourselves, but the tall and lanky owner of the shop could see us hiding in the stacks.

"Hello, Grace and Emmie," said David. "Grace, I got in the copy of that out of print Victoria Holt novel you asked for."

"Great."

Emmie kept one eye on the cafe while I got my book. I'd forgotten about it. I hadn't had time to read much lately anyway.

"Is Drew working on that ballerina murder case?" David asked.

"Yeah, he is."

I chatted with David for a few minutes while Emmie pretended to browse the shelves. Then he walked over to her.

"Emmie, would you be interested in our next literary art show? Artists paint something from literature. We usually have a theme."

"I've heard about those and seen pictures on social media. They look like lots of fun. I loved the Shakespeare one."

As he started talking to Emmie, I took over as the lookout. I could hear their conversation vaguely, but I was more intent on looking at the long line at the cafe.

"You should think about it. Grace tells me you're an amazing artist."

"She's my biggest fan."

"We'll be doing another one in a couple of months. I have a couple of ideas in mind. H.G. Wells' 150th birthday is coming up in September. Emmie, could I get your email address?"

"Yes. That sounds really cool, David."

"Emmie, they're leaving," I said and headed toward the door. "Thanks, David."

I walked out of the shop while Emmie stayed behind to give David her email address.

They headed further down Broad Street. They only got something to drink. Coffee, I surmised, but it could've been smoothies.

"Why are we following them?" I asked Emmie as she came up behind me.

"We need some excitement in our lives."

They paused for a moment, and Emmie pulled me into the recessed entryway for Bing's hat shop. She started talking about the hats and raised her voice. I assume to make the two women think we weren't following them when we actually were.

"I love these hats," she said pointing to a wide-brimmed black hat trimmed with white lace. It looked like something that could've easily been worn in the Victorian era or in a big budget musical from the 1940s or 1950s. Another hat sported a veil. There were a few with feathers and a couple with huge bows. We had a couple of ladies at church who wore hats like these on occasion. These hats were fancy. They weren't like me at all. I wouldn't wear one in public, but I would've loved to have played dress up with those.

"Why are we looking at hats, Emmie?"

I watched as Anna and Irina crossed the street and got into a vehicle. It puzzled me since Irina supposedly hated this group, and Anna was the ballet mistress. I guess they could've been friends from Irina's time with the ballet.

"I could see Miss Ruby wearing that hat in the corner over there to church on Sunday. She loves hats with big bows," she said, ignoring my question.

I watched the vehicle pull out of the spot and turned my attention back to Emmie. I looked at the hat Emmie pointed out. She was right. Miss Ruby was an elderly woman who attended our church. She was always dressed to the nines, and unlike the other hat ladies who only wore theirs on Christmas and Easter, she wore one on most if not all Sundays. I would've loved to have seen her collection. She had quite a few of them, and she didn't repeat them often. Emmie was always talking to Miss Ruby about her hats, and we were standing in front of her absolute favorite hat shops.

I decided to text Drew. Maybe I should've done that before now, but I didn't think to.

"I seriously need one of these. We need to go inside. Have you ever been in here?"

"Emmie, do we have time for this? I know you'd rock the hat, but that's not the point."

"There is no other point," she said, ogling the hats.

"The point is we are working a case."

Emmie turned and looked at me. She tilted her head to the side and raised an eyebrow.

"Working a case?"

"Well, it sounds better than stalking."

She laughed.

"That's true. But they're gone so we're not on a case now."

"Those two women are fishy. I thought Irina hated the ballet company judging by the letter she wrote to the newspaper editor and all the things Beth had said. If she hates the ballet company so much, why is she walking arm in arm with one of its head honchos?"

"I have no idea"

"Don't you think it's odd that those two are so close?"

"If I take that job with the FBI, I might be able to buy one of these hats."

"Emmie, stop talking about hats and focus."

"I am focused. I have a great dress that I could wear with that hat in the corner. The one with the feathers."

"Fine. You look at hats, but don't drool on the glass. I'm going to try and figure out what these two are doing together. Drew is going to meet us at the restaurant."

Emmie looked up at me and grinned.

"Okay, so I'm guilty of loving a hat."

"Emmie, you definitely need to work for the FBI so you can buy that hat."

She smiled.

"Maybe you'll join me there."

I shook my head.

"Where? The FBI or in wearing hats? Not a chance on either account."

She laughed.

"Come on. Let's go get that burrito."

We walked past a few more shops including the bar with its windows covered in posters for upcoming events. Several of the glass paned fronts were decorated with yellow stickers of a "Happy" robot created by a favorite local artist who goes by the name Porkchop. Those stickers from his Happy campaign always made me smile. He put them in a lot of public places. I looked down and even saw one on a manhole cover as we continued walking down the sidewalk.

The restaurant was located in one of the many older and repurposed buildings on Broad Street. Despite the fact that Augusta was founded in the 1700s, and Broad Street was one of the earliest streets in the town, none of the structures were even close to being that old. A fire in 1916 ravaged the street and surrounding area, leaving nothing but ash and rubble behind. The structures in the rebuilt district were built as multi-purpose units, many with businesses on the lower levels and housing above. Some still served that purpose. In this building, the lower level's walls climbed high into the pressed tin ceilings with their charming crown moldings.

The locally-owned restaurant served some of the best burritos and nachos in town. And some of the eatery's charm was in its decor. The walls were lined with art by a multitude of local artists.

Not long after we arrived, Drew joined us in one of the booths at the back of the restaurant.

"So did you find out anything about Irina Meadows?" I blurted out as he was sitting down.

He didn't answer the question right away. He made himself comfortable and took a deep breath.

"Oh Drew, I'm so happy you could join me for lunch. How's your day been?" Drew mocked me in a falsetto voice.

I gave him my best saccharine smile in reply.

"My dear husband, how has your day been?" I batted my eyelashes in my best southern belle impression.

He shook his head at me and sighed.

"That's all I get is a sigh?"

I tried to prod him into telling me more.

"Maybe I should ask you why you were following them. What did you plan to do if they spotted you?"

I looked at Emmie and shrugged my shoulders.

"We weren't following them. We were downtown and so were they. We were walking this way. We just took a little longer getting here that's all."

"Uh huh," he said skeptically.

Now, it was my turn to sigh. He wasn't playing well with others at all.

"This is an ongoing investigation, Mrs. Ward."

"Give us a break, Drew," Emmie said in a deadpan tone.

"Why did we see Irina and Anna together just now?" I fired

off another question.

"Okay. Okay. Yes, I spoke with Irina about two hours ago. I didn't find out too much that you didn't already know except that Irina and Anna are sisters."

"Sisters?"

I looked at Emmie. That was intriguing and odd all at the same time.

"Irina admitted she hated Aleksandra because she took her place after Irina fell and broke her ankle. That was about 15 years ago, which puts Aleksandra at about 18 when it happened. She stepped into Irina's spot. Irina was getting old for a dancer. She was 38 at the time and after years of abusing her ankles, her last injury didn't heal properly. Irina could never come back from it. Irina moved to the United States about 10 years ago and became a naturalized citizen. She worked with several ballet companies in the Southeast before meeting a wealthy businessman who'd pursued her after seeing her on tour in Europe years ago. She moved to Aiken about four years ago. She's part of several boards in Augusta and Aiken."

"Why didn't she want the company her sister works for coming here?"

Drew shrugged.

"She didn't have great answers to my questions, and she only has a shaky alibi. Supposedly, she was at home in Aiken during the afternoon. No witnesses to corroborate."

"What about her sister, Anna?"

"I'm not sure where she was. She claimed to have been at the hotel taking a nap. And of course, none of the dancers will admit they were anywhere near the theater around the time Aleksandra was killed. They all claim to have left around 1:30 and didn't return until around 5:45. They said that Aleksandra was still on stage when they left. Everyone we've talked to says that. She was practicing her pirouettes or something. That wasn't unusual. She was driven to perfection."

"No one is just going to admit they hated her and strangled

her to prove it," Emmie chimed in.

"Did Anna hate her?" I asked.

"Anna didn't say. She said their relationship was strictly professional. She claimed to have no feelings toward her one way or the other," Drew said.

"Yeah, right," said Emmie.

Drew smiled.

"A guilty conscience and a confession would be nice about now. There's not a lot of evidence lying around."

"You'll find out who did this, Drew."

Our lunches were ready quickly, and Drew ate like he hadn't had a meal in months. I knew he was in a hurry.

"Do you have to go back to the theater today, Grace?"

"I have to take flowers for tonight's performance. Aleksandra's orchids will be part of the flowers for the memorial service tomorrow so there really aren't any special requests for today."

"Let me know if you see anything suspicious, okay?"

His statement surprised me.

"You're asking for my help?"

I smiled, and he shook his head.

"You and Emmie were spying on two of my suspects a few minutes ago so you're going to help me whether I ask you or not."

"Oh, I almost forgot. I had a strange interaction with Natasha this morning. I went to the Riverwalk, and she found me there. She basically said she hated Aleksandra and was a better dancer. But she insisted she didn't kill her."

"Yes, she fed me the same lines yesterday."

"And one more thing - "

I didn't get far into my thought when Drew's phone rang.

"I have to take this. I'll catch you later," he said.

He got up and left the restaurant.

"What were you going to tell him?"

"About the sketch. I guess it'll have to wait. I had gotten so distracted with our Russian sisters that I didn't think about it until it was too late."

"I think you need a hat, hon," Emmie said.

"I need to get back to the shop."

"You take the fun out of everything."

"Speaking of the sketches, have you heard anything back from the FBI?"

She shook her head.

"It hasn't been that long."

"I just hope this doesn't hurt your chances with getting the job with the FBI."

"I really don't have anything to lose by sending the photos to Agent Monroe. I trust you and what you see, Grace. You saw me wearing ugly clothes and shoes and sketching. That means there's something else out there for me to do, and if it's not with the FBI right now, that's okay. Not that I want to leave you, but you know I love my art. I've always wanted to do something with that talent, and what you saw just lets me know I'm on the right track, honey. It's okay."

"Do you think he'll do anything with it?"

She nodded.

"I do. And I'm sure I'll hear something before long. You made a positive impression on Agent Monroe."

"Thanks."

"No problem. Besides this could be a break in the case. You never know."

She smiled.

"Come on. I want to look at that hat one more time."

# 7

When I got back to the shop, Jazzy had completed all of the memorial bouquets, and she'd gotten the flowers ready for the evening performance. She also did a couple of amazing "get well soon" arrangements. I wondered about the performance. I guessed Natasha would take Aleksandra's place. She was the understudy after all. It surprised me that they would still dance tonight and that they scheduled a make-up performance for the same weekend. The old adage that "the show must go on" was true at least in this case. I decided to look one more time on the Internet for something. I didn't know what. Anything that would shed some light on who these people were. Natasha was a mystery to me. I decided to try a search on her name. I had been focused on Irina and Aleksandra the day before, and Drew had interrupted my search.

Several Russian sites popped up with Natasha Ivanova's name. And some of them were quite interesting. Did Drew not know about these?

I found a gossip site that I could translate from Russian to English. She was a stereotypical redhead with a fiery temper. She'd been arrested once after a fight. She'd been with another ballet company and apparently, a reviewer said she looked like a "rhinoceros in pointe shoes." He commented that she was "bulky and ready to charge."

She broke his nose.

I laughed at the commentary.

But it was the second article that disturbed me. It was from seven years before. She was 25 at the time. She had been suspected of throwing acid in the face of another dancer because she didn't get the role she wanted. The charges were later dropped for lack of evidence. The attack had taken place at night, and the dancer didn't see her attacker. Everything was circumstantial. Fortunately the victim wasn't blinded, but she did suffer from burns to her face requiring extensive plastic surgery.

I tried to search out the name of the injured dancer, but other articles came up in French and German. I was able to get a translation of them, but it turned out they were the same article I'd just read. It left more questions than answers. One final article was about the dancer five years after the attack. She'd moved to a tiny village in Russia; no ballet company wanted her because of her face. She would never dance again.

I could hear Natasha's voice ringing in my ears. I could hear her telling me not to believe what people told me. She was implicated, but nothing was proven. On the other hand, just because she wasn't convicted didn't mean she wasn't the one who threw the acid.

I took several screen shots of articles and sent them to Drew. I also printed out copies as a backup. I could bookmark it on my computer, but if I wasn't in the shop then it wouldn't do me any good.

Drew didn't respond right away, but when he did, it was a simple "thanks, babe."

I needed to get back to my work and leave the crime solving to Drew. There were still things that had to be done, like preparing the two dozen red roses with a single red rose, trimmed in ribbon and tucked into the bouquet for the soloist to give to her dance partner. And there were a few arrangements that needed to go to the hospital.

But when I came out of my office, I found that Jazzy had already taken care of everything.

As I was standing looking at Jazzy's work, Beth surprised me by coming to the shop. She wasn't supposed to be coming today. Emmie was scheduled to take the flowers to the theater with me while Jazzy watched the shop. Beth waltzed into the flower shop and folded her arms across her chest. She didn't say anything. She just stood there, with a smug look on her face as she tapped her fingers against her arms waiting for me to ask her a question.

"So why do you look like the cat who caught the canary?"

She kept grinning and moved her hands to her hips. She tilted her head to the side.

"You know, I really should get something for being such a good citizen and providing the police department with so much help."

"So, what kind of juicy gossip have you learned since last night?"

She shook her head.

"No, no. This, hon, is much better than gossip."

"What are you talking about, Beth? Are you going to just stand there grinning at me?"

She walked back out of the shop, leaving Jazzy and me to stare at each other.

In a few minutes, she returned with a tall, lanky young man with thick blonde hair and a pronounced Adam's apple.

"This is Sergei," she said, still smiling.

"Dobryy den," he replied.

Jazzy and I exchanged glances.

"Dob-what?" Jazzy asked.

"That's Russian for 'good afternoon,'" he explained in a thick accent.

"Sergei is an exchange student. He's been living with one of our neighbors this school year," Beth interjected.

Someone who spoke and read Russian and could eavesdrop on what the Russians were saying. Pure genius. On impulse, I hugged Beth as tightly as I could. She seemed shocked. Beth wasn't a hugger.

"Beth, you're a miracle worker. Could I borrow him?"

"Of course. That's why I brought him here."

"I'd like to see American law enforcement. I'm interested in studying the law when I return home," he said.

"He's been here since last August so he's learned American English quite well," Beth said.

I smiled at Beth.

"Dobryy den, Sergei," I tried to say that with my Southern accent. I'm sure I butchered it. Sergei smiled back and nodded at me.

I thought back to the photos on my phone. Maybe that would be a good place to start all of this.

"Are you ready to start?"

"Of course," he said.

He looked confused and glanced at Beth.

I pulled out my phone.

"Grace Ward, do you have photos from the crime scene on your phone?" Beth asked in a high-pitched tone as she moved toward me to look at my phone.

I pointed my finger at her.

"Not a word, Beth. None of you."

"Yes, ma'am," said Beth.

"I also have a photo of the card I had to send with the flowers that I was delivering when I found the body."

I moved away from them as I searched for the photo of the card which Drew had taken into evidence.

"Here's the card."

Sergei took my phone to look at the photo.

"Counting the minutes until we're together forever," he read.

That was sweet, and it would make sense especially after my dream.

He handed it back so I could scroll to the next photo of the dressing room mirrors. I hesitated before handing him my phone again.

He wrinkled his brow.

"Traitors must die."

"Traitors must die?" I repeated slowly.

He looked puzzled and nodded.

"Yes, traitors must die."

I wondered what that meant.

"Listen, I have to go to the theater shortly to deliver flowers, and I have to go again in the morning. Would you go with me? I'd love to have someone to eavesdrop on their conversations."

"Spasibo," he said.

Aleksandra had said that to me. It meant "thank you." I wasn't sure why he was telling me that.

"That's 'thank you' in Russian," he said in response to my confused look.

"I know, but why are you thanking me? I need to be thanking you."

"I want to see your police at work."

I smiled.

"And no thanks to Beth?" Beth interjected. She stood with her arms folded against her chest and raised her eyebrows.

"Oh Beth, I don't know what we'd do without you, and you know it."

She laughed.

I made a quick call to Drew.

"Beth found someone not affiliated with the ballet who speaks Russian."

"Why does that not surprise me? Maybe I should just call her the next time I have a murder investigation."

I laughed.

"So did you get him to translate the message on the card and the message on the mirrors?"

I paused. How did he know?

"What are you talking about?" I feigned innocence.

"I know you, Grace, and if you didn't take pictures of the mirrors and that card, I'll resign from the sheriff's department immediately."

I took a deep breath.

"The message on the card said 'Counting the minutes until we're together forever,' and the one on the mirror said 'traitors must die.'"

I waited for Drew's response, but there was none. After an awkward few moments, I continued.

"I'm going to take our Russian friend with me. When people don't think you can understand what they are saying, they drop their guard and say things they probably shouldn't."

"That, babe, is very true. Call me if your Russian translator picks up anything, and I'll see how soon you can go to the police academy."

I laughed uneasily.

"I'll let you know if we find out anything."

I wasn't sure if Drew was happy with my information or not. We'd decided that Sergei would pose as my delivery truck driver. I gave him a baseball cap and a T shirt, and I told him not to say anything. That accent would give him away immediately. We didn't need anyone knowing he could understand them. I didn't think anyone would ask, but if they did, Sergei would pretend he had laryngitis.

We were going to try and linger as long as we could. I was going to fake needing extra instructions on the memorial service the next morning to give Sergei a chance to eavesdrop.

As I walked into the theater, the memories of Aleksandra's dead face flooded me. I felt a little short of breath. I stopped and nodded to Sergei that I was fine. I just needed to take a few deep breaths. I noticed a few of the dancers standing in the small space between the dressing rooms and the stage entrance. I walked out toward the stage to see if I could find Vladimir, the company's artistic director. He was the one I needed to ask about the flowers.

Sergei followed close behind me. I didn't see Vladimir on the stage. As we made our way back through the wings, a wafer thin dancer approached me.

"I need to apologize for my friend for yesterday," she said in broken English. "She was rude. She did not like Aleksandra. She should not have asked so many questions."

"Your friend?"

"Natasha."

I nodded.

"Did you like Aleksandra?"

The dancer smiled.

"She was beautiful when she danced. She moved on air. I wanted to be like her. I'm Elena," she said putting out her hand for me to shake it. She had a bubbly personality. She seemed like one of those people who would talk to anything that would listen.

"It's nice to meet you."

"I like to meet Americans. I am working on my English," she said. She had a thick accent. Fortunately for me, she spoke slowly and emphasized her words.

She seemed young and eager. It bothered me that she was so thin. I'd never seen anyone with thighs that slender, and it was easy to see them in her short chiffon skirt that hardly covered her pink tights. Her thighs were size of the average woman's calves. Her collarbone was so pronounced, and her hands were skeletal. To be so young, she looked so old.

"No one is saying how she died. There is much talk, but we do not know the truth."

"I can't answer that question. I don't know either. They have to do an autopsy to find out for sure. Was your friend the only one who didn't like her?"

"But you found her, yes."

"Yes, I found her, but I'm not an expert so I have no way of knowing how she died."

She nodded.

"My friend? Yes, Natasha. Natasha has temper. Aleksandra would yell, but only when it wasn't perfect. She wanted it to be beautiful. She did not get angry at us - only pushed us to get better."

"Did she yell at Natasha?"

"Yes, Aleksandra yelled at Natasha a lot. Natasha was injured in a performance not long ago - accident. She slipped and fell during a pique circle. There was a slick spot on the floor. She almost hit Aleksandra and tripped her. Natasha almost lost her job."

I nodded.

"Aleksandra was furious. She wanted Vladimir to remove Natasha. Vladimir calmed Aleksandra. He is so good at calming angry people."

"Do you think Natasha could have been angry enough to hurt Aleksandra?"

"Natasha? No, no, no, not at all. She has temper, but she would not hurt anyone."

"Was Aleksandra mean?"

"Aleksandra was a perfectionist. She wanted every dance, every movement from everyone to be perfect all the time. She encouraged Vladimir and Anna to give us extra rehearsals. She made us tired. But Aleksandra wasn't bad person. She was very nice person, most of time."

I nodded.

"Who could've killed her?"

She smiled at me.

"We all want to know. There were others who did not like her. She often brought shame on Anna and Vladimir."

"I don't understand."

"Shame. She shamed them. They would tell her to do one thing, and she would do her things her own way. Her way often looked better. This brought embarrassment to both of them when she did not respect their judgment. They felt it made them lesser in the eyes of the dancers."

As we were chatting, I heard a sharp voice in Russian. Elena looked away.

"I must go," she said.

It was Natasha, and while I don't understand Russian, I do understand body language. The red-haired ballerina had her eyes narrowed at Elena. Her jaw was clenched as she seemed to spew venom in a foreign language. Elena flinched as Natasha pointed a finger almost in her eye.

"I told you not to listen to stories. Don't listen to anything she says. She talks too much," Natasha said as she pushed Elena in a direction opposite me.

She narrowed her eyes, and her stare bore holes into me. Natasha said something in Russian and turned away, grabbing her fellow dancer's arm. Elena winced. She waved at me as Natasha continued to scold her. It didn't seem to bother her much. Sergei walked toward the opposite side of the stage with me. We kept our voices low. He'd been listening in on my conversation with Elena as well as the interchange between Elena and Natasha.

"What was that all about?" I whispered.

"Natasha called Elena several names. Elena said Natasha was overreacting and said Aleksandra had gotten what she deserved. She was a cow in pointe shoes. Natasha said Elena should take care in what she says or she might end up like Aleksandra."

I stared at him. Too much drama for me.

"Did she say something about me?"

He shook his head.

"Not nice what she said."

"I figured as much. You're not going to give me a clue?"

"I'm not sure how to translate to English. What she said is slang for stupid, fat woman."

"Thanks, Sergei."

It was interesting that Natasha had found me at the river and tried to convince me she was innocent although she did a poor job of it. Elena had plenty to say about Natasha and Aleksandra's relationship. And with everyone telling me not to believe anyone, well, maybe they were all right. I felt a headache coming on. I wasn't sure how Drew dealt with people like this on a regular basis. I was used to people who were basically honest. I didn't know how to deal with liars and murderers.

I told Sergei to leave the flowers on a table next to the stage door. There were two additional floors above us with dressing rooms. I thought I'd check upstairs to see if we could find Vladimir. I turned on my voice recorder on my phone. I had a hunch that we might be able to find something that could give Drew some clues as to what took place here.

We headed up the stairs. On the second floor, there were several dancers in pink tights and black leotards, warming up. We made our way to the top level. We paused outside the stairwell door. It was open, and I could hear loud voices in Russian. It was a man and a woman. I assumed the man to be Vladimir. I wondered who the woman was. She sounded older so I was thinking it was Anna, the ballet mistress. I looked at Sergei. He nodded. He seemed to be drinking in every word they said. He smiled a couple of times and then shook his head. I tried to keep quiet so he could hear them, but I really wanted to interrupt and get him to tell me what they were saying. Their voices continued to rise. Then there was no more talking. I had been right. It was Anna who stormed past us as though she didn't see us. I peeked around the corner to see Vladimir leaning against the painted cinderblock wall. He had covered his face with his hands and was weeping.

I cleared my throat.

"Pardon me," I said. "I wanted to find out if you needed anything else for the flowers tomorrow."

I'd startled him. He looked up at me and tried to pretend that he hadn't been crying. He nodded.

"Two more dozen lavender roses with the sparkle," he said.

"You mean the sequins added to them?"

"Yes, make them sparkle as Aleksandra would've liked."

"I'm sorry about her death."

"You found her?"

"Yes, I did."

"There's no one like her. These Americans won't know the difference as Natasha takes her place, but I will know. The Russians in the audience will know too. Natasha is radiant, but she is not the jewel."

"Yes, I knew Natasha was her understudy. Does she need anything special for tonight? I brought red roses."

"Nothing special."

He didn't look at me as he spoke in a monotone. As he said that, he walked past me and headed down the stairs. I wondered what he'd do with the lavender roses.

He shouted something in Russian as he descended the stairs to stage level.

"He told them warm up was in five minutes," Sergei whispered.

I really wondered what Vladimir and Anna had argued about. I guess I could find out soon enough. I stood back. I wasn't sure what to do. I didn't want to leave, but I did want to know what they were arguing about. From backstage, we could leave the dressing room area and go into the balcony seating. Maybe we could sit in the back and watch them warm up. I didn't have tickets to the performance, and this was probably as close to it as I'd get.

I motioned for Sergei to follow me. We could hear the dancers in the stairwell as they made their way down from the floor below us. There was a roar of Russian mixed with French as Vladimir barked out his instructions to the dancers. We moved down one of the landings and paused until there was silence. Then, we went through the dressing room area to the balcony stairs. When I thought we were far enough away from where anyone could hear us, I turned to him to ask about what we'd heard.

"What was all that fighting about?"

"Did you record it?"

I nodded. I handed him my phone, and he had a pair of ear buds to listen to the conversation.

"She was berating him for his affair with Aleksandra and for the way he acted with other dancers. She said not to worry about the performance that Natasha will be beautiful. She called him 'husband,' but she was angry when she said the word."

"Husband?"

He nodded.

"She said she loves him despite his faults and straying. She said she will take care of it and him. He doesn't need to worry. She will always be there. He protested. He said he never had an affair with Aleksandra. Anna didn't believe this. He said he loved Aleksandra, but he never touched her. Vladimir said he didn't understand why she didn't believe him - why she never believed him."

I looked around and saw a box near the stairway leading to the balcony. It was a box of playbills. I flipped through it to see the biographies of Vladimir and Anna. They weren't married according to their bios. There was nothing to indicate that they were a couple. They each dedicated their seasons to their mother land. I guess that wasn't considered important. But sometimes, people thanked their significant others in their bios or called them their inspiration. There was nothing like that. I looked under Aleksandra's bio. She wasn't attached to anyone either, according to the program. I wondered what their relationship was.

I tiptoed up the stairs and into the balcony. It was dark in the theater except for the stage lights and some low level house lights. I hoped no one would see us.

Vladimir was nowhere to be seen. Anna led the dancers in a series of stretches at the barre. She shouted out a long list of ballet terms. I caught her saying "plie" and "tendu." I recognized those two from my limited ballet training. I guessed this was the same stretch they always did before their performances because they all did the same thing without missing a beat. Despite their simple attire of a leotard and tights with leg warmers covering them, they were elegant, stunning in their moves. I sat mesmerized watching their flawless graceful poses as they carried out the moves. Their arms were held tightly in their strict movements, and their heads tilted. Their legs and feet obeying Anna's commands.

After several minutes at the barre, they lined up off stage.

"First group, tombe, pas de bouree, glissade, saut de chat," Anna shouted.

The dancers burst from the wings with their moves which included an athletic yet graceful leap in the middle.

I hadn't paid much attention to Sergei as I sat watching the dancers. I wondered if he liked dance, but he seemed to be watching them intently.

"Are you bored?"

"Oh no," he said. "I like ballet. My mother was a dancer, and I took ballet when I was a child. I was part of a traveling ballet company. This isn't my first visit to the United States. I was here when I was 11. We toured the country. Our bus was in an accident, and I shattered both of my ankles."

"I'm so sorry."

"No worries," he said. "I could never return to the stage. I wasn't flexible any more with the pins in my ankles. But while I was in the hospital and physical therapy, I watched your American crime shows. That's how I became interested in your criminal justice system."

"Well, I'm biased. I think my husband is the best at what he does, and he works with a lot of really good people."

"I'm excited to learn," he said.

I stood up.

"I don't think we're done here. I can't give you a reason. I just think there's something else."

"Thank you for bringing me."

"Thank you for being my spy. Come on, let's see if we can get anything else."

I hung around trying to think of some reason to still be there. I was running out of reasons, but no one said anything to me. No one shooed me off. We stayed through the rehearsal. It was beautiful. As the dancers dispersed, we walked back to the dressing room area one last time. Aleksandra's dressing room was still cordoned off with police tape.

"Natasha," I asked as she headed to the dressing room.

"Yes?" she looked at me suspiciously.

"You looked lovely out there. Do you need anything for your dressing room tomorrow- flower wise, that is? I know Aleksandra had specific things she wanted."

"No, thank you. Red roses are perfect."

I didn't know what I was waiting for, but I was sure I'd come away with some snippet of information if I just stuck around a little longer. The husband and wife thing was good, but I wanted to impress Drew with my detective skills. He was right. I was going to help him whether he wanted me to or not.

I guess the next thought was what Drew would call a hunch. There was another exit in the stairwell in the backstage area. I wasn't sure why, but I motioned for Sergei to follow me downstairs.

"What are we doing?" he whispered.

"I'm not sure. Let's just hang out for a few more minutes, okay?'

He nodded.

After about 15 minutes, we heard voices. I wasn't sure if Russian naturally sounded angry or what, but these voices started softly and kept rising. By now, I knew what Anna sounded like, and I was pretty sure she was talking to Elena. I started recording what they were saying.

The interchange didn't last long. I heard two sets of footsteps. After the silence, I motioned again to Sergei, and we headed to the delivery van.

"What was that all about?"

"That was odd. The older woman - what was her name?"

"Anna."

"Yes, Anna said that Elena had gotten them into a huge mess. Everything must be fixed or they would be in deep trouble. Someone else could end up like Aleksandra. She sounded like she was threatening Elena."

"How were they in trouble?"

"She said Aleksandra was going to cost them a lot of money. Elena - that's what I heard her called. Elena said she had plenty of contacts and not to worry. The money would be there. She did not have to worry. Elena started to get angry. She told Anna to never threaten her again. She said her friends were powerful and dangerous."

Well, that was cryptic.

I called Drew and told him everything that had happened. He wanted me to take Sergei with me in the morning to the memorial service, and then he'd use his language skills to find out what was really going on. They hadn't been able to locate any Russian speakers not associated with the case. I drove Sergei back to the house where he was staying.

# 8

It had been a long day. I knew Drew would be at the theater for a while, and I needed to step away from everything. I decided to drop in on my parents. I took my mother flowers from my shop from time to time. She loved flowers, and I brought her a few of Aleksandra's orchids. My visits were probably going to be less frequent soon. My brother, Zack, and his brood would be transferring to Fort Gordon within a few weeks. I'm sure my brother's kids would be visiting their Nana quite a bit in the next few months especially with the new baby on the way. I was probably going to schedule fewer visits to her house so that our paths didn't cross.

I had to shake this feeling of failure. In my head, I knew that not having a baby didn't mean I was a failure. This was the 21st century. I hadn't let all of womankind down because I wasn't a mother. I wasn't even sure where this thought came from. Drew didn't make me feel like I was a failure, neither did my parents or any of my friends. It was crazy to me, and no matter what I told myself, I couldn't shake it. Not having a baby at my age made me feel like I was less of a person. Being around my brother's family would accent those stupid feelings I couldn't get rid of. I'd be comparing myself to his wife, Sarah, and mentally feel like I'd lost. Thanksgiving and Christmas were going to be hard. Those were two days I wouldn't be able to avoid them all. Maybe Drew was right. Maybe I really did need someone to talk to.

My mother was sitting on the porch when I arrived. It was almost as though she expected me.

"What beautiful flowers," she said.

She smelled them and walked into the house.

"I have just the place for them."

I followed her in and looked around.

"Where's Daddy?"

"Oh, he went down the street to check on the Greens. Mr. Green broke his hip and just got out of the hospital."

I followed her into the kitchen. She was flitting around the house as she usually did. She couldn't stay still for more than a few minutes at a time. She always had to be doing something, which was another reason I was surprised to find her out on the porch. The kitchen smelled good.

"Are you staying for supper? There's some chicken casserole, collards, and stewed tomatoes and rice. Your dad ate right before he left. I made enough for them to have for tomorrow. But I still have some that I just put away."

"I'm not - "

I started to say hungry, but before I could get the words out of my mouth, my mother was standing in front of me with her hands on her hips, staring at me and shaking her head.

"You've lost weight, and you're too pale," she announced.

I nodded.

"You're getting too thin."

"I'm fine, Mama."

"You need to sit down and eat. I've already put it away, but it's labeled in my refrigerator. And I can get it with no trouble."

I knew what that meant - lots of plastic butter containers with dates written on masking tape. That was her refrigerator filing system. She opened the refrigerator and started pulling them out. She made a plate for me and stuck it in the microwave.

"It won't take a minute to reheat it."

"I'm fine."

I should've known better than to protest. She wasn't listening to me anyway. And I'd better eat the food when she put it in front of me.

"No, you're not. I talked to Drew this morning when I heard about the ballerina."

"Yes, I did the flowers for her."

"And what else?"

"What do you mean?"

"What aren't you telling me?"

"I had a dream."

"You've always had those, and they've helped a lot of people. But you're jumping all around the question."

"So, you wanted me to tell you that I found her body?"

I was confused at this point. Just what was she trying to get out of me? With that statement, however, she left her being busy around the kitchen and came and sat next to me. "Oh my Lord, bless your heart, sweetie. What an awful thing to happen to you. Twice in two months even," she said.

"I thought you knew and that's why I couldn't figure out what you were asking."

"No, it's just a mama's intuition to know when something's wrong with her baby."

"I'm not a baby, and I told you I'm fine."

"I know you aren't fine, and I know you are an adult, but you'll always be my baby. You might be able to fool other people, but you can't fool me. You can hide stuff some of the time, but not all. I have lemon pound cake. That's just the fix."

"Are you sure Emmie and I weren't switched at birth?"

"What on earth are you talking about?"

"You and Emmie think food is the answer to every problem."

"No, that's prayer, but food helps while you're praying."

She was serious. I knew her. I really wanted to laugh, but that would hurt her feelings. As I was trying not to laugh, my father walked in. He walked up to my mother and gave her a quick peck on the cheek then he walked over and kissed me on my forehead.

"Good to see you, honey," he said.

My mother had walked over to the refrigerator and pulled out the sweet tea. She poured him a glass and forced it into his hands.

"Drink this. Don't be getting dehydrated on me. I don't need you having a heat stroke," she said.

"It's only a couple of houses down. It was a good walk, and it's not that hot. You're overreacting."

"Drink," she said.

"Thank you, Lottie Lou."

She just shook her head at him.

My mother's name was Charlotte, but she'd always gone by "Lottie." The "Lou" on the end was a family joke of sorts, dating back to her childhood. My mother's best friends were Mary Louise, also known as Mary Lou, and Cindy Louise. Yes, she was also called "Cindy Lou" so to make them a trio, they added Lou to the end of my mother's name. She never really liked it, but some people called her that all the same. I think after all these years it had just stuck so she made the best of it.

I thought about the lemon pound cake. Lottie Lou's Luscious Lemon Pound Cake was what she called it in the church cookbook, and it sounded wonderful about now.

My mother and grandmother had always seemed to think that food was the answer to many of life's ills. They were great cooks. I was not. But they never showed an ounce of the pound cake or biscuits on their hips. Like Emmie, my mother had a great metabolism. I must've inherited mine from my dad. She was always watching his weight. Her pound cake was the only food item that had actually sounded good, and I usually loved her chicken casserole.

"Could I just skip supper for the pound cake?"

"That's not good for you. Have some real food first. Those tomatoes came out of my garden. They're some of the first I've picked. I got the collards at the Farmer's Market," she said as she placed a piping hot plate of chicken casserole, tomatoes and rice, and collards in front of me. I had to admit it did look good, and it smelled heavenly. Everyone was right. I hadn't been eating, but this food definitely got my attention.

"It smells wonderful."

"Tastes wonderful too," my dad said. "I had some earlier, but I'd love another piece of that pound cake."

"You've had enough for one day, Jackson. Now go. You made it home in time for your show. Leave us girls to talk."

"I'll be back. Don't eat it all, Gracie," he said.

She gave him the look that she meant business, and he went about his way. Then, my mother sat down next to me and gave me that same look.

"So tell me what's wrong," she said.

I knew I had to answer that look. I shook my head and looked down at the plate.

"Just seeing their faces, Mama. Both of the women. I don't think I'll ever be able to get them out of my mind."

She sat down next to me and took my hand.

"What does Drew say about all this?"

"That I need to find someone to talk with."

"I think he's right. You should listen to him."

I nodded at her without saying anything. I didn't want to interrupt her.

"Drew's a good man. He's always watched out for you."

"I know he has."

"And I know he's been going through a rough patch, but that's all it is. It's a patch, and he'll make it through as long as you believe in him."

"He seems to be making progress."

"But?"

How did she know these things? I didn't tell her. And I know Drew was quiet.

"But I think he's only dealing with the symptom and not the root. He still refuses to talk about Mark and Linda."

"Did you know that Dana and Bill Andrews were separated?"

I shook my head. I was shocked. Why did she change the subject? I guess I knew where I got that from.

"No, I sent her a note to let her know I was thinking of her, but I ... "

My voice trailed off. Some friend I was. I was so consumed with my own life that I left my friend hanging out to dry. I hadn't visited her since her baby was born and now her husband was gone. More guilt to add to the pile.

"She heard about the many things Bill had been involved with - the women, the parties, the drugs. She's concerned about the baby."

"Bill used drugs?"

"Not used, sweetie, sold."

I really had been in my own world.

"What? I'll admit I always thought Bill was a lowlife, but a drug dealer?"

"Well, you don't think he's a great businessman, do you? How do you think he kept up with his lavish lifestyle? He's done all kinds of things, and you know it. He's headed to bankruptcy court and probably jail before it's all over."

"I'd heard he was under investigation, but I didn't hear anything specific. I'm surprised Beth hasn't said anything. I'm sure she knows."

"I'm surprised Drew hasn't said anything to you."

My mother raised her eyebrow at me.

"Mama, you know Drew doesn't talk to me about a lot of things. I know that, and I'm fine with it. I don't need to know everything that goes on in this town, and there are a lot of things I do know that I wish I didn't."

Mama shook her head.

"I'm sure that's wise in a lot of ways. Sometimes, ignorance is bliss especially when you can't do anything about it."

"I still can't believe that Bill was a murder suspect in Drew's last case. After what I heard then, I suppose I shouldn't be surprised at this. Do you think he killed our ballerina?"

"I can't imagine what for."

"I was joking, Mama."

From there, the conversation lulled. My dad came back in after a few minutes to get a piece of lemon pound cake so there was no talk of babies or my brother or murder. She sat and watched me eat and scolded my dad for eating too much. The pound cake was amazing. It melted in your mouth, and there was just enough sour to go with the sweet.

We talked about the weather and flowers. And then, she took me out to her garden. I think my love of flowers came from my mother. Our quality time when I was a kid came around planting tomatoes or transplanting potted plants into larger pots. We spent a lot of time getting dirt under our fingernails. She didn't like to use gloves. She liked to connect with the soil. She said it kept her in touch with nature, and it kept her humble.

She talked for a few minutes over the fence to her neighbor, Stefanie, who uses the container garden method in her yard. They compared notes on how their various plants were performing while I listened to the interchange. I missed having a garden, but there wouldn't be one this summer.

Before I left, she wrapped half of the pound cake in tin foil and put it and some other leftovers in a plastic grocery bag. I thought about protesting, but it was useless. I wouldn't win. I could take the pound cake to the shop in the morning. Emmie loved it.

Surprisingly, I was home by 8. I wasn't sure how long the performance was, but I hoped Drew would be home soon. I knew he was still looking for the killer. I wondered what he'd found, and if my information helped him any.

Rain had started drizzling on my ride home, which cooled off the temperature. Sitting outside at my mother's house had made me want to sit outside once I'd gotten home. I loved the smell of the rain. The shower didn't last long though. I rocked on the front porch swing and listened to the sounds of the frogs and crickets. I watched as the night sky twinkled from the lightning bugs in my yard. Even though it was only May, those were the sounds of summer in Augusta.

I thought about summers past as I sat there. My brother and I would catch the lightning bugs and put them in a jar with leaves inside it, and we'd poke holes in the top of the lid. I liked them in their free state now as they flew from my azalea bushes to the trees and then vanished into another yard. If I stayed out long enough, I might hear the owl that sometimes showed up in the yard. But it would have to be really dark before he made his presence known. Sometimes, I saw a random bat looking for mosquitoes or at least that's what I hoped it was looking for.

Life seemed so much simpler in summer - at least it did as a kid. No school, no worries. My mother was home with us. We made trips to the library every few days to get books, and we went to the lake. We spent hours in the park. I could feel the tears rolling down my cheeks as I remembered those days. I wanted to do that with my own children. With the things I'd seen in the past couple of months, I wondered what meaning my own life really had. Two young women were dead. The FBI agent on the last case told me I'd helped save many lives by assisting with the case, but what about the ones that had been snuffed out before my help? And what about the ones who were still alive, but their lives were wrecked because of what they'd gone through? There were moments when I looked at Jazzy, and she seemed to not be there. Even with her counseling and the front she put up, I wondered if Jazzy was having problems adjusting. I wondered if she was afraid that something would happen to put her out on the street again. I wondered if she really trusted us or if she thought that maybe we'd taken her on as a pet project that we'd drop once we were bored with her.

I silently prayed as I sat on the swing. I prayed for God to hear me and help me. I prayed for that baby I'd seen in my dreams. I prayed for Jazzy and for Emmie, and I prayed for Drew to catch this killer.

Once again, my thoughts drifted from one subject to the next much like a bee in the spring, collecting pollen from one flower and flying off to the next one.

I wondered how Drew dealt with this. He had handled most deaths with ease, except the deaths of his two friends. That one he wasn't handling well, but he seemed to be able to cope with the rest. He might not have been a homicide investigator for long, but he dealt with death on a regular basis - car accidents, domestic violence. There were countless things I knew he didn't tell me, but I'd read about them in the paper or watched them on the news. I knew we were safer with him and others like him on the job, but I didn't know how they did it.

I moved from the swing to the top porch step. There I could gaze into the heavens as I listened to my frog and cricket chorus. It was a cloudless sky now so I easily spotted Orion and the Big Dipper, but that's as far as my astronomy knowledge took me. I wondered how the ancients saw the pictures they did with some of the constellations. Yes, my mind darted from place to place. Drew, Emmie, and the others were right. I needed someone to talk to; someone who wouldn't say anything, but someone who would just listen to me. I needed someone who would let me ramble on. I knew my friends would listen to me, but I didn't want to be a burden to them.

I closed my eyes and heard the slam of the screened door behind me. Drew sat down next to me.

"What are you doing out here? I thought you'd be inside working on my case."

I laughed.

"Thomas Andrew Ward, I have given you enough information on your case that you should make me an honorary deputy."

He laughed.

"You aren't far from the truth."

"Besides, I didn't think you wanted my help - or Beth's or Emmie's."

"I appreciate everything you've done. You've helped more than you know."

"So then, what have you found out from what I've fed you?"

He raised an eyebrow at me and winked. He kissed me. He could be infuriating, but those blue eyes. I still found myself melting in them at times.

"You're changing the subject."

"I know. I like this subject much better."

He kissed my neck.

"Did you arrest anyone?"

"Not yet."

"Are you going to tell me anything?"

"You don't let me get a word in."

I held up my hands in surrender.

"Fine. My lips are sealed."

"Just some hunches right now, but I think that something will happen at the memorial service tomorrow. This group has more drama than ballet. It's like a soap opera. With the information you gave me, I was able to put together some interesting pieces. And your little friend, Elena, spilled the beans on the backstage antics."

"That's not surprising."

"So Vladimir and Anna are married as you found out with your eavesdropping. Hardly anyone knows it because they don't tell people. Apparently, they have some open marriage type agreement where they don't put ownership on each other. At least that's how Elena phrased it. And Vlad lived out his side of the bargain to the fullest according to her. From what Elena said few people have resisted him."

"Gross. He's bald and fat and smells like," I stopped. I didn't know what he smelled like, but it wasn't pleasant. I'd gotten close enough to him to realize that."He smells like garlic or something. Yuck. I don't want to even think about that."

Drew laughed.

"People will do all sorts of things to get what they want."

"I'll do things, but I won't do that. Nothing is that important to me."

"I'm glad to hear it."

"Besides I only have eyes for you, Drew. No one else ever has come close to you. That was my promise to you. I've kept it this far and intend to keep it 'til death us do part."

He leaned over and kissed me again.

"Okay, what else?'

"I'd rather kiss you than tell you about all of this."

"You can kiss me later."

"Thanks, babe."

I laughed.

"No problem. What else?"

He smiled as he shook his head and continued.

"Vlad has had relationships with a lot of the dancers including Aleksandra according to the gossip. Everyone knew about his relationship with her. It was a long term one, but he even cheated on her."

"What does he say about all this?"

"He claims they didn't have a sexual relationship."

"And what man is going to admit to that especially if he's married to someone else?"

"True."

"Did you see that scar on his forehead? Apparently, it's a reminder from Aleksandra that he'll always have. She threw one of those crystal vases at him."

"People kept saying she threw vases, but she didn't seem like the vase-throwing type. Although if they were having a fling and she found out he was married, I could understand her throwing a vase. She would've had to have been really strong though. Those things are heavy, especially when they're full of water and flowers."

"Yes, she packed a wallop from what I understand. Who knows who was telling the truth about any of this? For all we know, Anna could've beat him over the head. Anyway, things were iffy with them during their romance. But apparently, she came back from the season break last summer and told him it was over. He denies the relationship, but I can tell he's not telling me the entire truth. What's a lie and what isn't - that's what I'm trying to find out. Apparently, she barely even spoke to him this season. They didn't even talk about the weather; they didn't have any interaction except about her dance. Elena said she thought it was just because Aleksandra had hit the ultimate diva state. Aleksandra had decided she didn't need anything but her talent, and she certainly didn't need Vladimir. This opened the door for Natasha who took Aleksandra's place."

"Does Vladimir have a temper?"

"Oh yes, he has a doozy of a temper according to several dancers. He's verbally abusive, and he's also been known to throw things at them as well. And he's a heavy drinker. He's the stereotypical Russian vodka abuser. And from the sounds of it, I'm sure the sexual relationships with the dancers weren't always consensual. But that's another case."

"Great, so everyone has a motive and opportunity. Anna hated Aleksandra for the relationship with her husband; Natasha hated Aleksandra because Aleksandra had the role Natasha wanted; Vlad was upset about the breakup. And Irina just had old grudges she couldn't put down."

"That sums it up," Drew said, nodding at me.

"What about our chatterbox?"

"Elena?"

I nodded.

"She's inconspicuously conspicuous," he said.

I laughed.

"What do you think Anna was talking about to Elena? About the money and all and then Elena threatening Anna?"

"I have no idea. Unless there are sponsors who might pull out because of Aleksandra's death."

"But who would Elena know?"

"I can't answer that."

"Is there any forensic evidence?"

"You'd think this was a crime of passion, spur of the moment, but it seems to have been well thought out. They're testing for DNA evidence. It looks like the killer could've worn gloves though. No one has any type of scratches or bruises, and there didn't appear to be any skin under Aleksandra's nails. Plus, the fingerprints you'd expect to find in the dressing room weren't there. Aleksandra wasn't the only person from the ballet company in that room. Other people went in and out. We found their prints on the door, but not really anywhere else. Vladimir, Anna, and Natasha's prints are on the door. Yours are too. But not in the room; it's weird."

"Of course, they are. I was there, and I touched the door and maybe the counter?"

"There are a lot of prints in there because the auditorium sees so many acts coming through. There are a few famous ones as well."

As I thought about the concerts that had been at the Bell recently, I could only imagine. They had brought in a slew of famous people.

"So prints only on the door. I guess that is strange, but she did tell me she was lonely. She probably didn't have too many people in her dressing room."

"Not on the chairs or mirrors or costumes. Very odd. I think the killer wiped everything down."

I took a deep breath.

"What's next?"

"I want you to take Sergei with you and see if there's any more chatter."

"I'd planned on doing that anyway. Sergei seems excited about it, but he really wants to meet you and see what you do."

"I'd like to see if he'd translate for us once we get everything we can. Elena didn't mind talking to us one bit, but it was harder getting information out of some of the others. These Russians plan on leaving soon so we've got to nail this down."

"There's supposed to be an after party for the sponsors tomorrow night. Are they leaving Saturday?"

"First thing. Is that all you have to tell me, Grace?"

"Isn't that enough? I think I've told you everything I know. The strange flowers and note in Russian. The writing on the mirrors. The man in my dream. You know - that stuff."

He nodded and paused before he furrowed his brow and turned to look away.

"Have you left anything out?" he asked me.

"Me? I don't know what you mean."

I was honest when I said that because this had been a long and exhausting day.

"I got a call from Frank Monroe today."

"Oh."

"So you did leave something out."

"Not intentionally. I'd forgotten all about it. Emmie sent him the sketch, but I didn't put her up to that. She did it on her own."

"I didn't say you did."

"She thought about facial recognition software, and that the FBI probably had it. I wasn't sure what type of technology you had access to."

He nodded.

"Did he find anything?"

"The mystery man, if he exists, doesn't have a criminal history and isn't wanted in connection with any open cases in the U.S., if that's what you mean. He doesn't have a driver's license registered here either. Running it through other databases could take a while. But the main thing is we don't know if that person exists. And if he does exists, who's to say that he's even American? He could be European for all we know, and that would be another database."

I didn't say anything, but I didn't like the way Drew kept saying "if he exists." I knew he was a real person, and Drew's comments were making me angry. I had had too much experience with my dreams to think that this man was a figment of my imagination. I stood up so I could head toward the door. I was too tired to start an argument.

Drew reached out for my hand.

"I'm sorry, Grace."

I turned to him.

"I'm not arguing with you, Drew. Do you know why? Because he is real. Emmie showed me the drawing she'd done of the man Vladimir described, and they look alike."

"Why didn't you tell me this before?"

"I don't know. I've been so busy. I tried to tell you at lunch, and you got called away. I haven't had time to think about anything else. I'm tired, I'm frustrated, and I'm scared. I want to know what's going on in your world but not this way."

He stood up and pulled me close to him.

"This will be over soon, and you and I can spend some time together. Just you, me, and the beach," he whispered in my ear.

He let me go and stared directly into my eyes. The light from the full moon in a cloudless sky danced in his eyes.

"Frank Monroe didn't tell me there were two sketches, but he did tell me he's going to keep looking 'til he finds something."

He smiled. That last comment showed me he was remorseful. That he at least regretted saying those words to me. He was smiling at me now. He wasn't as angry about my dreams as he had been. Things were changing for the better, and I needed to focus on the good. At least, he didn't head straight for the liquor bottle when he got home. I tried not to be too irritated with him. "And thank you, Grace, for all your help with this. You've given me genuine leads that I could follow up on. "

I nodded.

He winked at me and gave me a mischievous grin. I wasn't sure what was coming next. He leaned down and kissed me softly, gently. This I could handle, but what he did next I wasn't ready for. His lips trailed down my neck to that one ticklish spot. He knew exactly where it was. I should've known. I loved for him to kiss me there, but at the same time, I hated it because I hated being tickled. And it had been such a long time since he did that. I began laughing uncontrollably.

"Drew, stop."

I tried to wriggle out of his arms, but he continued to kiss me. I laughed so hard that tears started pouring out of my eyes. It was always the strangest sensation to be crying and laughing at the same time.

After what seemed like forever, but was only a few seconds, he stopped and looked at me. I was still laughing through the crazy tears. He let me go, and a serious look came over his face. I took a deep breath and calmed down.

"I love to hear you laugh," he said, but he wasn't smiling as he should've been with a statement like that. "And you don't. Since Christmas, you just don't laugh anymore."

He was right. Laughing felt good even if I was tormented by the tickling. I hadn't felt much of anything in months. I moved forward and pressed my body against his. I wrapped my arms around his neck and drew his face close to mine, kissing him with a passion that I hadn't felt in weeks.

"I think we should go inside, Grace, or somebody might call the police," he whispered in my ear, before scooping me up and carrying me inside.

# 9

I saw the darkened stage. In the center was a portrait of Aleksandra. I couldn't see much -only an outline of her face and a pale light reflecting from it. In the shadows, I could see other faces. There wasn't much detail to them, no definition. I stood in the center, and I rotated 360 degrees From the stage, I looked into the house. It was dark where the audience would sit; not even the row of safety lights was lit. As I stood on stage, a light began to appear. It looked like the glimmer of a match, but then it grew. I could see someone standing in the back. It was a faint image. A silhouette cast in the shadows. Fuzzy, gray.

A voice cried out her name. Over and over in an anguished cry, a male voice called her name.

A light shone on his face. It was him - the man from my previous dream.

I wondered what his accent sounded like. For some reason, I couldn't make it out. He was Russian, wasn't he? Maybe he wasn't.

Then I was in the balcony, and he was alone on the stage. In his hand, he held several lavender roses wrapped in white tulle. He knelt in front of the portrait and touched it as tears streamed down his face.

I woke up with a jolt. That was all too real. Drew wasn't lying beside me. I looked at the clock. It was almost 6:30. I walked outside in my pajamas - a tank top with pajama pants. They weren't revealing so I didn't care if the neighbors saw me in them. I found Drew back out on the front porch sitting in the swing with a cup of coffee. He seemed to be lost in thought as I stepped outside to sit next to him. My biggest event of the day would be Aleksandra's memorial service, and that wasn't scheduled until noon. The flowers were all ready to go.

"I'd forgotten how nice it is just to sit outside," Drew said as I joined him on the swing.

"It's one of the main reasons we bought this house and not a newer one, and we hardly ever sit out here anymore."

"Yes, I remember. You insisted on a front porch and old trees."

I nodded.

"I like a house with character."

"This one is definitely a character."

Drew shook his head.

"Oh, you know you love it as much as I do."

Yes, the house had more than character. It definitely seemed to be a character at times. It was a picture perfect house on the outside. Inside, it needed some work. We didn't have a huge budget to save it from all of its woes. The plaster was cracking on some of the walls and the plumbing - oh the plumbing - you didn't want to go there. The pipes were as old as the house, I think. It squeaked and squawked for various reasons. The furnace needed to be replaced. It was an antique. But overall I loved the house and its quaint front porch. It oozed the South to me. We used to spend a lot of time together on the porch when we first bought the house. We'd eat our dinners outside in all kinds of crazy weather. It had great trees including a huge oak that shielded the home from the effects of the sun, and it had a cute, monkey grass-lined brick walkway from the road. A couple of the bricks were stamped with "Augusta" on them. There was a hedge of azaleas. It was my little paradise.

"I just wish I was more of a handyman. There are so many things I'd like to do with it."

"I know."

We had done some remodeling when we first bought it. The house was built in the 1920s and had many occupants over the years. When renovating the floors, we found some small children's toys in the floor boards. There were a couple of jacks and a rubber ball, and in the attic, we found some newspapers from the 1940s tucked away. One had a headline for DDay. I'd saved the papers and framed them. I wonder what the walls would say to me about those who'd lived here before me. These things made my house my cozy abode.

I snuggled next to him and rested my head on his shoulder, thinking about our sweet house. Late spring mornings were warm but not hot. There was a breeze blowing. It felt good against my skin. We used to sit on the swing a lot in the first few years after we moved in, but we'd been so busy lately. You could sit outside for most of the year except maybe a few days in January. At Christmas, I liked to decorate the porch with a small Christmas tree and lots of multicolored lights.

"Grace?"

"What's the matter?"

Once again, I'd drifted off into my own little world. I was oblivious to the fact that he'd been talking to me the whole time.

"Would you do me one favor?"

"Sure."

I hesitated when I said it. I'm not sure why. It wasn't like he was going to ask me to do anything difficult.

"Would you delete those photos from the crime scene from your phone?"

I nodded.

"Sure, I don't need any dead bodies on my phone."

He did a double take.

"You mean you took pictures of Aleksandra's body too?"

Apparently, I'd left out that part. I nodded again.

"I didn't tell you that?"

"No, you didn't. Why would you do such a thing?

"I can't answer that."

"Let me see those."

"I didn't touch anything."

"I know you didn't, but let me see them anyway."

I went back inside and found my phone, unlocking it and scrolling to the photos before handing it to him. He took my phone and stared at one of the photos, enlarging it before shaking his head.

"What's the matter?"

He glanced up at me.

"You know that I can't go on your dreams as evidence. It helps that Vladimir may have seen someone that resembled your mystery man, but I have to tell you that upfront."

"Yes, I know."

"What did you tell me about the man in your dream?"

"That she was obviously in love with him. And he was definitely not Vladimir. He was the total opposite. He looked fit and had jet black hair which wasn't really short but wasn't long enough for a pony tail either. It had a few waves in it. He had distinct facial features."

I paused.

"What?"

"I had another dream about him  last night. He was in the theater."

Drew looked back at the picture and shook his head, handing me the phone. I looked at the portion of the picture he'd enlarged. It was Aleksandra's hand. She was wearing a large diamond solitaire on her left hand. I looked up at Drew to find him staring at me.

"She was engaged?"

"No one has come out with that information, so I don't know the answer to that. Everyone said that she was unattached as far as they knew."

"That rock definitely looks like an engagement ring to me, and it's on the correct finger."

"Yes, a pricey one from the size of it."

"Well, you and I both know there's some serious money invested in this ballet group."

"Yes, there is, and there's something strange about that that I haven't been able to put my finger on yet. Grace, did you ever see this man who was in your dream?"

I shook my head. I'd run through that over and over in my mind. When I had the dream, I wondered if maybe he was showing up in my mind because I'd seen him. And when Emmie drew him for me, I knew that I'd never seen him before.

I smiled. I was confident he'd show up in a database somewhere. I was sure he wasn't American so the fact that nothing had shown up in the U.S. database didn't surprise me.

"If she was engaged to our mystery man, then that could've been the reason she broke things off with Vladimir months ago."

"That's a good possibility. Let me see your pictures again."

He scrolled back and then he looked up at me again.

"What now?"

"When did you take these other photos of the make-up counters in the dressing room?"

"When I went to meet with the theater's management. That's right before I met Aleksandra - alive."

He kept moving from one photo to another.

"What's wrong?"

He handed me the phone.

"Grace, how long was it between your first visit to the dressing room and the next one when you found the body?

"I found the body close to 5, and I had gone to the theater around 10:30 in the morning. So it was most of the day. Why?"

"Look at those two photos and tell me what you don't see."

I felt like I was playing one of those games where there were two photos side by side and you had to find the differences. But then it hit me.

"There was a gorgeous tiara in a clear box on the counter top, but I don't see it in any of the other photos."

"And I don't remember seeing it when I was at the crime scene either."

"You think the murderer took it?"

"This sounds a little like Cinderella. Find the missing tiara and you can find your killer."

"That's not the greatest analogy," I shook my head and laughed.

"But you get the idea."

"Yes, I do."

"What time are you going to the theater this morning?"

"Probably around 11 with Sergei and Emmie."

"Beth doesn't want to go?"

"She's going, but not with me. I think a few people from the area arts' groups are coming, and since she's on a bunch of boards, she's going to represent them at the ceremony."

"If she sees anything, let me know. If Beth is one thing, she's observant and nosy. Well that's two things. That'll help me out."

As we sat on the swing, I noticed someone walking down the sidewalk and stopping at our gate. It was Jazzy.

Drew gave me a kiss.

"I need to go. I'll see you in a couple of hours."

"Okay. Go catch some bad guys."

He smiled.

"Good morning, Jazzy," he said as he headed to the car.

"Good morning, sheriff."

"I'm not the sheriff," he said with a laugh.

I stood up and walked to the porch steps.

"Good morning, Jazzy."

She didn't have her usual peppiness this morning.

She waved as she walked down the path to the house, but her shoulders were sagging, and she didn't have a smile on her face. I walked down to meet her. She had to have been hot. Beth lived about three miles away. She didn't say much. She just tried to give me a weak smile.

"Come inside."

I led her into the kitchen.

"Do you want something to eat?"

"I'm all right," she said. Her voice was listless. Her Cajun twang wasn't so twangy today.

"Does Beth know where you are?"

"Probably not."

I sent Beth a quick text. I didn't need her to be worried. I poured her a glass of orange juice and put it in front of her. I wondered if I'd been right about everything I'd been thinking last night.

"Thanks," she said without looking up.

"I have cereal and some fruit. I think there may be some bacon left. I need to go to the store."

She shook her head and stared at the orange juice.

I grabbed a bowl and spoon, the cereal, and milk and put it in front of her then I sat down.

"Do you want to talk about it?"

She shrugged her shoulders a bit.

"Miss Beth is kinda strict and Miss Emmie - she's the opposite. You seem to be in the middle."

"Okay, I'm not sure I know what that means."

"Well, you're more like my mama than the other two. And today would've been her birthday. I miss her."

Jazzy started to cry.

I slid my chair a little closer to her and put my hand on her arm. I didn't say anything. I wasn't really sure what to say. I figured I'd listen. After a few moments, she dried her eyes and started to talk.

"I know things are changing for me, and I appreciate everything you're trying to do for me. I still don't know why y'all are being so nice to me. No one has been nice to me since my grandmama and mama...."

"Jazzy, when we were stuck in that warehouse together, I felt like I got to know you. I've always prayed for the chance to really help someone, and that someone is you. I'm glad you're in our lives."

"I just don't know if I can do it."

"Do what?"

"School and make something of myself."

"You can do it, Jazzy. There are a lot of people who believe in you, and before long, you'll start believing in yourself."

"I want to believe. Four years living on the streets. You don't know what that does to a person. You're treated like you're nothing but a piece of meat. No one wants you - not the real you. No one cares. It's hard to trust. I wake up in the morning and wonder when reality is going to come crashing in."

"It's over, Jazzy. And we're going to help you so that it never happens again."

I put my arm around her as she continued to sob.

"I have these dreams at night, and I can see my mama. She keeps telling me that she loves me, but I just feel like I've let her down. Her and my grandmama too."

"You didn't let anyone down. People let you down, but we're going to fix that. Okay? You've been doing great things at the shop. You have made some really cool designs, and you've made some customers really happy. You have a gift for making people feel cared about, and you don't even realize it, Jazzy. I  know you're going to go to school for something in the medical field, but you have a great eye for design. I think you'd make a great interior designer."

"Really?"

"Yes, really."

"I've always liked colors and fabrics. I've been in some nice hotels and some really ugly ones."

"You'd be great at that."

"They don't have that at Augusta Tech."

"No, they don't, but you can start somewhere now. No one is locking you into one career for the rest of your life. Most people don't do that anyway. They start in something and find out what really suits them."

"I'm excited about the medical stuff, but I don't know if I'll be good at it. I'll probably be thinking about changing out the art work or paint colors in the offices."

I laughed.

"You sound like Emmie when you say that."

"Miss Emmie is amazing. She's so talented."

"Yes, she is."

"You know, I feel like my mama has been watching over me, and she led me to you."

I smiled.

"Maybe so. You know, Jazzy, you haven't spent much time with my mama, but I think you'd like her too. She makes a killer lemon pound cake."

She smiled.

"I love lemon pound cake. My grandmama made the best."

"Would you like some for breakfast?"

I laughed. I don't think my mother would approve. I knew that wasn't healthy, but for some reason, it sounded like a good idea.

"Yeah. I would."

In that moment, I saw the child in Jazzy come out. With all she'd gone through, she'd been denied a childhood, and there were times when she fought to reclaim what she'd lost. I realized that maybe something good had come out of Drew's first murder case. Jazzy wasn't being trafficked any more, and she was going to have a good life. I knew things were only going up for her. And she wasn't the only one.

"This is really good," she said as she took a bite. "My grandmama's was the best, but your mama's comes a close second."

I just smiled.

# 10

I showered and got dressed, and Jazzy drove in to the shop with me. Beth dropped Sergei off at the shop and Emmie met me there to help me load the flowers into the car. Besides the memorial bouquets, there were several arrangements from other dance and arts organizations in town that needed to go to the service. We needed to arrive at the theater about an hour before the memorial was set to begin. It was quiet even though some of the dancers were there. They were wearing leotards and tights as if they were going to be warming up for a show. The female dancers had their hair slicked back into disciplined buns. There was not a stray hair to be seen. They were also wearing theater make-up with thick eyelashes and lots of mascara. I guess no one was planning on crying during this memorial. I wondered what kinds of words would be spoken, and if she really was hated. I'd gotten such mixed messages on her.

There were bouquets for the women dancers and single roses for the men. Anna and Vladimir as well as other crew members traveling with the performers had flowers. Sergei carried in some of the larger arrangements for us. We placed all the flowers on a table in the theater's wings. The dancers were supposed to pick up their bouquets as they passed onto the stage during the service. A full-length framed portrait of Aleksandra was placed center stage. I had an email telling me where to place the flowers. There would be a single spotlight on the photograph during the ceremony. I put her signature orchid in a champagne glass beneath it, and Sergei placed a couple of free-standing wreaths on either side. I stepped back to take a better look. Emmie walked up next to me. She nudged me with her elbow before folding her arms across her chest.

"I think we did a fantastic job if I do say so myself."

"Two of those four arrangements you did so yes, I'd say you did a great job as always. I hate to see you leave me."

She smiled.

"You know you can't get rid of me completely, and nothing is definite yet."

She hugged me.

Sergei stood near us, watching and listening as a few dancers took a moment to approach the portrait before the ceremony. They whispered in Russian to each other. I turned slightly to see Sergei shaking his head to signal that their conversations didn't really mean anything. Elena, the skeletal busybody ballerina, walked over to the framed photograph. She kissed her fingers on her right hand and touched the picture. She lingered for a few moments as she stared at it. Natasha walked up behind her and said something rather loudly. Elena turned to look at her. Tears streamed down her cheeks as she pushed Natasha out of her way. Sergei touched my arm and leaned over to whisper in my ear.

"She said, 'Traitors die' and you could end up just like her if you're not careful."

I wondered what she meant by that. I sent Drew a quick text. I knew he'd be in the theater soon. Sergei and I milled around backstage until time for us to distribute the flowers. There were a few whispers among the dancers. I watched as a few dancers glanced at Natasha and turned away quickly. Their body language indicated that she was most likely their target of conversation. I looked for Sergei. He made himself look busy as he weaved among the dancers to listen in on their words. After several minutes, he returned to stand by me. We walked out into the lobby, and he told me what he'd heard.

"Two of the dancers were talking about fights they'd seen

between Aleksandra and Natasha especially the night after she'd fallen and almost caused Aleksandra to fall," he said. "Other dancers talked about how glad they were that the season was almost over so they could get away from Vladimir. They were heading to other ballet companies and new jobs."

"I wonder if that's what they mean by 'traitor.'"

Sergei shrugged his shoulders.

"There was also talk about money and how only a few people in this group saw the money. They were complaining about that."

I thought about Natasha's "traitor" comment. She certainly looked strong enough to strangle someone. She was tall and although she was thin, she had well-developed triceps and biceps unlike Elena who was so emaciated looking that she probably would blow over in a heavy breeze.

The memorial was set to begin in a few minutes, so we moved into the wings. For safety purposes, the stage wouldn't be completely black the entire time.

As we gave the bouquets to each dancer, I looked into their faces. There were some, like Elena, who shed a few tears. Others looked angry, and others showed no expression at all.

"I loved to watch her dance," Elena said as she passed through, picking up her bouquet and smelling it, while wiping tears away.

I watched as Natasha came to pick up her bouquet. She didn't say much. She looked more worried than sad to me. I wondered if she thought she'd be arrested. If I was voting on a killer, she'd get my vote, but Anna was bulky too. Vladimir? He definitely could've done it. I think I judged every dancer who walked by. Who knew what really went on behind closed curtains?

Natasha walked to her spot on the stage, but Elena didn't stand next to her. She kept her distance. I wondered what had happened between the two of them. Maybe Natasha had found out the things Elena had said about her or maybe Elena thought Natasha was the killer after all.

After handing out the bouquets, Emmie, Sergei, and I headed to the balcony. I wasn't sure why we were sticking around. I didn't think the ceremony would be in English. They were Russian dancers, after all. Sergei sat between Emmie and me so he could tell us what was going on. It wasn't long before Drew joined us as well.

"So you must be our Russian interpreter," Drew said.

"Da," Sergei said and nodded. "That's Russian for 'yes,' and yes, I am."

"Are you ready for what could be a long afternoon and evening?"

A wide smile spread across Sergei's face.

"Da. I want to see this firsthand."

Drew smiled at him and patted him on the shoulder.

Just like everything the Russian dancers did, the memorial service was artistic and visually striking. And it was eerily close to my dream. The dancers stood in a semi-circle behind the portrait. A single spotlight shone on the painting as the silhouettes of the dancers fell into the shadows. They were all dressed alike and held the same pose in ballet's first position. The women wore black tights, black camisole leotards and short black chiffon skirts with the men wearing all black as well.

It was odd in May to hear the sounds of Tchaikovsky's Waltz of the Sugar Plum Fairy playing. The music conjured up memories of Christmas tree decorating and shopping at the mall. The Nutcracker seemed to be every store's soundtrack of Christmas.

On a white screen above the dancers' heads, a swirling image of Aleksandra in a glittery pink costume and sparkling tiara played. Elena was right; she was beautiful. At the end, a beaming Aleksandra bowed several times as the audience erupted. That wasn't the only video. I'd never seen anyone do so many spins at one time. It made me dizzy just watching her, but it was hard to take your eyes off her. She was graceful, but at the same time, there was a degree of athleticism as she effortlessly jumped across the stage. It was mesmerizing. I could only imagine what she looked like live on stage

Vladimir was the first to speak. While the ceremony was mainly for the dancers, there were others who'd gathered to show their support. I saw Beth in the crowd. I assumed the crowd was filled with representatives from arts groups. I recognized some of her friends who were also my regular customers.

Vladimir spoke in English for the benefit of those non-Russian speakers gathered.

Vladimir called Aleksandra "a unique talent."

"She was born to dance," he said. "Every part of her was wired to dance."

I'd see Vladimir go from stoic to hysterical when it came to Aleksandra's death, and he remained true to form. Vladimir broke down during his eulogy. Anna stood next to him to console him.

"Our company will never be the same with her gone. She was the greatest dancer I've ever worked with. There will never be another Aleksandra -"

He couldn't go on any longer. He choked in the middle of her name, overcome by his grief. He shook his head and covered his face. He cried as he walked off stage.

I wondered what Natasha thought of that. I couldn't see her on the darkened stage. The dancers were like soldiers. They didn't move. They didn't flinch even when she was hailed as the greatest dancer. They kept their position.

After Vladimir finished, the dancers were allowed to say a few words. Several of them came forward. Not surprisingly, Natasha was not one of them, but Elena was.

She said a few words about how beautiful Aleksandra was and how she admired her. Then she said something loudly in Russian and bolted off the stage in an awkward run. It was not ballet-like at all. Sergei sat stunned. He turned and looked at Drew.

"She said she's ashamed of the dancers because she knows one of them is a murderer, and that they are cowards. But she also said she's afraid that one of them could be the next victim."

I watched as Drew left his seat and sped toward the back

stage. Sergei followed him.

Vladimir quickly returned to the stage to calm the dancers, and Emmie climbed over the seats to get next to me.

"Elena is overcome with her grief. Do not allow her feelings to interrupt this time," said Vladimir trying to regain control of the situation.

"Do you think Natasha is capable of killing?" Emmie asked.

"The motive is definitely there, but several people have motive."

"I wonder how her debut went last night."

"I didn't hear anything, but then again, who would tell me? These dancers are a tight-lipped bunch. They don't talk to the outsiders. And I didn't ask Sergei if he overheard anything about last night."

I wanted to know what Drew was up to, but I couldn't exactly follow him and get in on the interrogation process. Maybe Sergei would tell us later.

We sat through the rest of the ceremony. It wasn't what I expected. I thought there'd be more. Anna didn't speak, and I didn't see Irina in the small gathering in the audience either. The eulogies were over in a few minutes. When they were finished speaking, there was one final video of Aleksandra. She curtsied to the audience several times and then the video faded to black. The dancers placed their flowers below the portrait and in silent single file, they left the stage.

"Well, I guess that's it. It doesn't look like this is going to get Drew any closer to finding out who did this," said Emmie as she began to stand up. I had a feeling this wasn't over despite the quiet in the theater.

"Aren't you coming with me?"

"Not yet."

I spoke in hushed tones, and Emmie followed suit.

"Why?"

"I don't know. I think Drew might call it a hunch."

"What aren't you telling me?"

"Did you ever hear back from Frank Monroe?"

She nodded.

"I did. In everything else going on, I forgot to say something. He said he hasn't found anything yet, and they want me to come in for an interview soon."

I grabbed her hand and squeezed it.

"That's exciting, Emmie. You should do it."

"I am, sweetie. I am."

"Emmie, you can go, but I'm not leaving until... I don't know. I'm just going to sit here. Okay?"

"Well, you're the boss. And you're my ride. It's too hot and these heels are too high to walk back to the shop."

I smiled.

We sat in silence for several minutes. I watched as the small gathering downstairs began to dissipate. Close to an hour later, Emmie and I still sat in silence. I think Emmie had dozed off. They'd even turned the house lights completely off as the building was practically empty with the exception of us. I wondered where Drew and Sergei could be.

I sat watching the stage. The spotlight remained on. I wondered if this was what a stakeout was like - waiting around for something that might not happen. And then when I was ready to call it quits, it happened. A man walked out on the dimly lit stage. Emmie was asleep next to me so I elbowed her.

"That's him, Emmie. That's him," I whispered.

I jumped up out of the seat quickly and headed toward the exit. In that moment, I cursed myself for not moving closer to the stage, but I didn't want to be seen. He could be gone by the time I got there. I didn't know where Drew was, so I called him.

"He's on the stage, Drew. The mystery man is on the stage."

Of course, by the time I made it to the stage, he was gone. I ran across the stage and noticed a group of flowers that I didn't make. I knew every flower on that stage, and a bouquet of six lavender roses with some white ribbon with glitter on it was not one that I had made. I picked up the flowers. I wonder if he'd come in after I left. There was something about the bouquet that had "Jazzy" written all over it. I wasn't sure why. Drew and another deputy bolted out the exit. Had they seen him or were they just chasing the lead?

It wasn't long before Emmie and Sergei had made it to the stage.

"It was him, Emmie. The man in my dreams. He was real."

"Grace, you don't have to convince me. I knew he was real before. And yes, I did see him briefly. He heard us moving and rushed out the exit that Drew went through."

"This morning, Drew looked at my photos on my phone. She was wearing a huge diamond ring. I was so shocked that I didn't even notice it, and Drew didn't think anything of it when he saw her body."

"She was engaged, and that had to be her fiancé."

"How did we miss him, and why wasn't he part of the ceremony?"

"I don't know, but I believe this engagement was what got her killed. There's more to this than we realize."

"Well, we need to realize it quick."

I stared at the roses in my hands. There was a card.

"Sergei, what does this say?"

I held out the card handwritten in Russian. The flowers may have come from my shop, but Jazzy didn't write the card. And now my fingerprints were on it. Hopefully, there were others on it as well.

"It says 'until we meet again, my beloved.'"

I nodded.

Drew came back through the doors a few minutes later. He was on his cell phone. He shook his head at me. I guessed that meant he didn't find our mystery man. He walked up on the stage, and I could hear his conversation.

"Frank, whatever you can find out about the man in those sketches, let me know," he said before he hung up the phone.

"That was fast."

"He disappeared. There must've been a car waiting for him outside or something. There are a couple of deputies outside interviewing people. He's a ghost."

I held out the bouquet to Drew.

"I didn't make this one. He left it here, and he left this card. Maybe there are fingerprints on it or DNA or something."

He smiled and shook his head at me.

I didn't say anything although "I told you so" was definitely in my mind. He walked closer to me and gave me a big hug.

"I'll see what I can find out," he said.

He looked at Sergei.

"Come on. We've got more work to do."

Sergei grinned.

"Yes, I'm ready, sir."

"Grace, do you have to come back here tonight?"

I nodded.

"Do you need to go back to your shop?"

I wasn't sure if he was asking me or telling me that he wanted me to leave.

"Yes, I do."

"I'll see you later on. Okay?"

He leaned over and gave me a kiss on the cheek.

"I guess that's our cue to exit, Emmie. I need to ask Jazzy something anyway."

Emmie nodded.

"I'm starving though. We need to grab something to eat before we head back."

She looked at her phone.

"It's not nearly as late as I thought. It's not even 2 o'clock yet."

When Drew was out of earshot, I turned to Emmie.

"Do you still have that sketch on your phone?"

"Yes, I do."

Jazzy was full of smiles when we returned to the shop. I was glad after our breakfast earlier this morning.

"Girl, we've done some awesome business in the three hours you've been gone."

"Great, Jazzy. About that. Emmie, show her the sketch."

Emmie looked confused but pulled up the image anyway. I took the phone and showed it to Jazzy.

"Did this man come in here and order a bouquet of lavender roses?"

She took the phone and narrowed her eyes as she looked at it.

"Yeah, he had some kind of funny accent. I don't know where he was from."

"What did he say?"

"He told me exactly what he wanted in the flowers. Some guys come in here just wanting red roses. Or they want something else, but they have no idea what that something else is. He knew. He just spouted it out as he came in."

"How was he acting?"

"He was acting strange. He looked like he was gonna cry a couple of times. His eyes were red and puffy. I think he'd already been crying or he was drunk, but he didn't act drunk just sad."

She paused.

"He asked me who Grace was."

"Really?"

"Yeah, I told him you owned the shop, but you weren't here. He just nodded his head to let me know he'd heard me. I've had people ask me if I was Grace, so I didn't think anything about it. That's when I went into the back to get everything together. It only took a few minutes. The glitter ribbon was my idea."

"Did he tell you who the flowers were for?"

"No. Were they for that ballerina who died?"

"Yes, they were. He didn't say anything about what the flowers were for?"

"No, ma'am, only that they were for someone real special."

"We think they were engaged."

"Aw, that's so sad. I could tell he was tore up about something with all that puffiness going on. I just didn't know what it was. Sometimes I want to ask people, but I don't feel it's my place."

"I know what you mean, Jazzy. If they want you to know, they typically tell you."

I was hoping Drew would call soon. I wondered what his latest rounds of interviews had yielded if anything. I knew he was looking at the clock. The hours were ticking away. He needed something concrete to arrest someone before this group left town. I knew that it had to be someone in the company. Irina Meadows may have had a motive, but I really didn't think it was her. Fifteen years is a long time to harbor a grudge unless there was something else going on. Maybe she wanted to get revenge for her sister over her brother-in-law's cheating heart. Maybe that made her hate Aleksandra even more. Everyone looked guilty to me.

I still wondered about the man in my dream. I decided to try one more time to find information on the Internet. Why was it so hard to find information on a world-famous ballerina in this day and age? Well, in English anyway.

I sat down at my desk and put in a bunch of name combinations. I was so glad that the search engine recognized what I was trying to do, but giving me articles and sites in Russian without offering me a translation didn't help me.

"Do you need me to help you with anything?" Emmie had brought in a couple of sandwiches.

"No. Trying to find something on the internet about these people. Something that could give us the break we need."

"You're talking like Drew, hon. It's his case not yours."

"No, it's my case. He might be the official one in the books and the one who is getting paid to solve it. But it's mine. I can't help it."

"Well, I can't help you with your search. I came up with everything I could think of when you tried to look up Irina the other night. We searched for everything under the sun."

I typed in Aleksandra's name along with the word

"engagement." Nothing. No announcement. But the search also produced several ads for diamond rings. I wondered about hers. Was there anything special about it? I scrolled through my phone to the photo of her body. I hadn't deleted it yet even though I knew Drew wanted me to. I tried to zoom in on her hand. It was a large diamond. It had to have been several carats. We knew that her death wasn't associated with a robbery, but that piece of info sealed the deal. Anyone wanting to rob her would've taken that monster-sized ring. She couldn't have been wearing that on stage. She would have sliced her dance partner's face if he'd gotten too close.

"Wow, is that her ring?"

"Yes, it's massive."

"Her boyfriend would have to have a nice income to afford something like that rock."

"How big do you think that is?"

"Beth would know the answer to that one. Do an image search and maybe we can get an idea."

I pulled up a few photos, and from the looks of other images, that diamond had to have been at least 10 carats, maybe more.

"It's really odd that there's nothing about an engagement for her. She was a star in Russia, and he's obviously wealthy. A match like that is sure to cause headlines."

"Some famous people don't like being in the limelight."

"I know she was famous, but maybe he wanted to keep it quiet until the right time."

"Maybe, but I think there's more to this puzzle than we're seeing."

"I think you could be right."

"Listen, I've got to go and pick up the boys shortly. Car line is a beast. Do you need anything else?"

"No, Emmie. Thanks for your help."

# 11

I spent the rest of the afternoon doing paperwork and hoping to hear from Drew, but my cell phone was silent. I didn't have much to take to the theater for the final performance. My instructions were simple - a red-rose bouquet for Natasha with a single stem she could remove and give to her dance partner at the end of the show. There was no diva or rumor of one in the house tonight so nothing extravagant was required. They'd scaled back the sponsor after-party, and I didn't have too much to make for it now. After making the final delivery to the theater, I decided to head back to my shop. I needed to put the final touches on one large arrangement for the party and deliver it to the venue. I knew Drew wouldn't be home any time soon. I had some paperwork I needed to do as well. I'd neglected my receipts over the past couple of days with all of hubbub concerning the murder, and if we were going to be heading out of town soon, I needed to make sure everything was in order before I left.

Although it was nearly 7 o'clock, the sun was still shining and blanketing the front of the store. I entered from the back of the shop and walked through the work room. Jazzy had left everything as it should've been. I was in the backroom working on the centerpiece for the after-party's food table when I heard someone knocking on the door. I knew I'd put the "closed" sign out, and the store hours were clear. I was going to tell the person I was closed, but as I got closer to the door, I could see that it was no ordinary customer. He had jet black hair. His angular face had a pronounced nose and a dimpled chin. It was our mystery man. I stood frozen at the door, staring at his face. I'd seen him in my dream and I'd fleetingly seen him at the theater. And there he stood. He was real. I mean, I knew that he was, but it never ceased to amaze me when my dreams showed up in reality. And he looked exactly as I'd seen him in my dream. I was sure that I didn't see him before I found Aleksandra's body. I didn't think he was the one who'd killed Aleksandra, but I couldn't figure out why he was here.

He knocked again and held up his hands. I thought maybe he was trying to signal to me that he wasn't a threat. I felt like an idiot. I wondered how long I'd stood there and stared at him with my mouth open. I walked to the door and unlocked it.

"Are you Grace?"

"Yes. You speak English?"

He nodded. I supposed that was an odd question.

"I speak seven languages including Japanese and Swahili. English is my third language after French and Russian."

I smiled at him as I opened the door, so he could come inside.

"I'm sorry. I'm being rude. Please come in."

"I want to apologize for frightening you, but I assure you I didn't kill Aleksandra."

I nodded slowly. That was quick. This was an odd conversation we were having. Both of us knew things about the other person, but neither of us knew each other at all.

"Why are you telling me that?"

"You are married to the policeman, no?"

His accent sounded French, but it was faint. I was really confused now. I nodded in answer to his question.

"Yes, I am. Do you need me to call him?"

"No, I want to talk to you."

And it didn't make it any less awkward that we were still standing in the doorway. I locked the door behind me and then walked ahead of him. I wasn't sure how much I should tell him. Telling him that I'd seen him in my dreams wouldn't be the best answer to give him. That would make me sound a little strange.

"I came to you because Elena said I could trust you."

"Elena? Yes, I met Elena several times. She was quite talkative and seemed to love Aleksandra."

He nodded and smiled. This was getting more confusing by the moment.

"I don't understand."

"Elena's my half sister. I was born in France, and she was born in Russia. Our mother was a dancer. She had me when she was very young. It was hard on her career, but 15 years later, she married Elena's father. Elena was born soon after. Our mother and her father died in a tragic car accident when Elena was 14. I became Elena's guardian. She joined this tour a couple of years ago. They performed in Moscow and Kiev before coming to America. I met Aleksandra through Elena. It was love at first sight. I've been able to see her in several cities. I'm the artistic director at another ballet company. She was going to quit, join us, and marry me. Elena was going to join the company as well."

"And Vladimir didn't want to lose his star?"

"No, he didn't, but he didn't kill her."

"He wasn't angry that she broke off their relationship?"

He gave me an odd smile and raised an eyebrow.

"I see you've heard the gossip. None of that is true."

"Oh. I wasn't sure I'd believed it. Vladimir..."

I shook my head, and he smiled at me.

"Aleksandra was a talent all her own. She didn't need to sleep with a man to get ahead in her career. Her talent made room for her. She was highly sought after. And she didn't need Vladimir. Vladimir needed her."

I wished Drew was here. He needed to hear this, not me.

"Did you send the courier to send her the flowers a couple of days ago?"

"Yes, unlike what everyone said, it was the sunflowers she loved and the lavender roses wrapped in tulle."

He looked down as he said that.

"So why are you here? Do you know who killed her?"

He nodded.

"Yes, and I have proof."

"Why are you talking to me about it? Why don't you go to the police?"

He stared at me. All of a sudden I felt unnerved. I didn't know who this man was. He could've killed her for all I knew, and he wouldn't answer any of my questions. I'd put my purse down in the workroom. My husband had taught me to shoot, and I had a license for a concealed weapon. Of course, my gun wasn't close by. That seemed to be the story of my life. When I needed it, it wasn't close. And in this moment, that scared me. I wondered if I needed it.

"How do you know who killed her? And why did you come to me?"

I moved behind the counter. I don't know why I thought opening up the space between us would make me safer.

His face changed. His eyes welled with tears.

"I was going to meet Aleksandra in her dressing room between performances. No one was supposed to be in the theater but her. She didn't know I was coming. I was sending the flowers ahead of me so she'd have two surprises. She loved surprises," he paused and looked away.

"I got there early and waited a long time until I thought everyone had left. Vladimir seemed to be the last one leaving the building. I think he spotted me. I tried to hide, but he didn't pay any attention to me. About 15 minutes after Vladimir left, I could hear screaming coming from the window of Aleksandra's dressing room. I rushed to get inside, but I couldn't find a door that was unlocked. I tried several doors," he choked back tears.

He took a deep breath and tried to compose himself.

"When I got in, I could hear Anna and Irina laughing - cackling almost. It was awful. I came in one door, and they were heading out a side door. I rushed into her dressing room to find her on the floor, dead with the pointe shoes around her throat. As I knelt down beside her, I noticed her phone on the floor, smashed. I knew I didn't have much time. I took her phone and left. I walked to the door, and I saw your vehicle. The parking lot had been practically empty when I arrived. I didn't want anyone to see me so I stepped into the stairwell next to the dressing room. I waited until you walked right past me. And I ran."

Irina and Anna? Both of them killed Aleksandra? I didn't recall seeing Irina and Anna when I arrived, but I had stayed in my car for a few extra minutes to answer a couple of text messages before heading into the theater. And I know that I didn't see him.

He paused. He closed his eyes and shook his head. The tears continued to fall.

"I loved her. I can't believe they'd do this to her."

I wasn't sure what to do. I wanted to comfort him in some small way. I went from being afraid of him to wanting to give him a hug in no time. I reached out my hand across the counter to touch his. Maybe that wasn't the best move to make. Tears in a man did something to me. Most men I knew didn't cry often.

"I'm sorry. I didn't mean - "

"Thank you for your kindness," he said.

I reached for the box of tissues I kept under the counter, and I gave him a few. He offered a weak smile and cleared his throat. After another moment, he started talking again. He pulled out a phone with a cracked screen.

"She recorded everything on her phone. She liked to send me video messages. She told me that they were better than love letters, and I could play them whenever we were apart."

He stared at the phone while he spoke.

"Even though the phone is cracked, you can still see the video. She was in the process of making a video for me when they came in. She was showing me her engagement ring. We'd only gotten officially engaged about two weeks ago. She didn't wear her ring when performers were around. She kept it in a box. She was so full of life.

Then they stormed in and -"

He paused again, and he looked at me. I could see the pain in his eyes.

"Why did you wait until now? And why are you bringing this to me?"

He didn't say anything right away. He took a deep breath and glanced away for a moment.

"I have a confession to make. I've been following you. I've been afraid of your police. I didn't know what they'd do to me since I'm not from here. I don't know how your laws work even though I've visited here often."

"If you didn't kill her, then you would have no reason to be afraid."

"I've been a coward. I ran, but then I remembered what Elena said. She liked you. You made quite an impression on her. She said you'd help me. I realized after I ran from the police that I need to get justice for Aleksandra. I've been so stupid."

"Of course, I'll help you. Let me call my husband."

That gave me an excuse to get my purse. I didn't think I'd need my gun now, but I wanted it nearby. I walked back to grab my phone, and I noticed a missed call and voicemail from Emmie. It would have to wait for a few minutes. I turned around and walked back out into the shop, but he was gone. I walked to the door and looked around outside. He'd practically vanished into thin air. I glanced back at the counter, and there was Aleksandra's cell phone next to the unused tissues I'd given him. I wondered why he'd taken it from the scene. I knew I shouldn't touch it. I stared at it, wondering what to do.

I could feel my heart beating. It felt like it was in my throat. This was evidence. And it wasn't just any evidence. It was the evidence. It would put someone behind bars for a long time. I knew I should call Drew, but for the same reason I'd taken photographs at the crime scene, I had to see the video. I picked up the phone with the tissues he'd left. I felt so stupid. I'd given him a way to get rid of his prints, but at least I wouldn't leave any either. The phone was unlocked. I scrolled until I found the right video. I paused before starting it. I shouldn't be doing this. I took a deep breath.

Aleksandra was seated in front of her mirror. Of course, she spoke in Russian, and Sergei was not there to translate for me. I could tell she was a woman in love. She smiled broadly and flashed her ring at the camera. Her voice was melodic as she chatted away. She blew a couple of kisses. I wondered what she was saying. But as I watched the video, I realized that was the woman I'd met. She was vibrant and vivacious. Maybe love turned her into that person. He said they'd only been engaged a few weeks. Love could definitely change a person. Maybe she had been all those other things they'd said about her before she fell in love. I couldn't put those two images of her together.

It was a beautiful scene. She seemed to be saying goodbye, and as she was blowing kisses, two women barged into the room, yelling in Russian.

Aleksandra's face changed. I could see the fear in her eyes.

I had to turn it off. I couldn't watch any more. I was already seeing her dead face. I didn't need to have memories of her actual death. Tears began to fall down my face.

I needed to call Drew, but I had to regain my composure first. I checked Emmie's voicemail to give me that time I needed.

"Sweetie, I got a text from Agent Monroe. There's a hit on facial recognition software on our international man of mystery. Nothing came back in the U.S., but he's wanted in connection with some kind of smuggling operation in Europe. Frank didn't give me any details about what they wanted him for. I don't know if that means he was the smuggler or if he just has information about a smuggling operation. He hasn't been linked to anything in the U.S. yet. But Frank said if he's in the U.S., he's in the country illegally, using some kind of phony ID. He doesn't know if the man is dangerous, but I thought you'd want to know."

That would explain why he didn't go to the police and came

to me instead. I could pass on the evidence and get the two women arrested without him getting into trouble. I wondered if he was on the video and that was the reason he'd taken the phone. Maybe he'd erased something. I tried calling Drew, but he didn't answer. That wasn't surprising. I'd go to him instead. I grabbed a plastic bag and put the phone in it. I rushed out the door to the theater. I tried calling, but no answer. When I got there, the theater was crowded. There was no place to park. I drove around to the nearby James Brown Arena parking lot. Even it was full. I'd forgotten there was an event at the JBA as well as the Bell Auditorium.

I took a deep breath. I had to get in touch with Drew. On the next call, it went straight to voicemail, so I sent him a frantic text.

I know who did it. I have proof. Trying to find a way into the theater now.

I finally found a spot a couple of blocks away from the theater. I was glad I was wearing flats as I rushed along the sidewalk avoiding tripping over the uneven spots.

When I got to the theater, I wasn't sure how to get in. I didn't have a ticket. The throng of evening gown clad women and tuxedoed men mingled in the lobby, and the crowd spilled out the front door and onto the stairs leading to the theater doors. I heard smatterings of English and Russian in the chatter. With so many people at the door, I couldn't get up to the stairs.

I wished Drew would answer my text.

I headed down the side of the theater to the stage doors. One of them was opened, but I was immediately greeted by a security guard.

"I'm sorry, ma'am. You have to come in the front."

"I'm looking for my husband. He's with the sheriff's department - Drew Ward."

He radioed the others.

"What's your name?"

"Grace Ward."

"There's a Grace Ward for Investigator Drew Ward," he said

into his lapel radio.

I waited for a couple of minutes, and Drew came out of the dressing room area. I rushed toward him.

"Grace, what's up?"

"I've been trying to text and call you."

"I'm sorry, babe."

I held out the plastic bag containing the phone.

"The answer is in here."

He looked confused.

"This is Aleksandra's phone."

"Did you take this from the crime scene?"

"Are you serious? No, Drew, of course not. The mystery man showed up at my shop this afternoon. Just take this."

"The mystery man?"

"Yes, the one from my dream; the one who was at the memorial service. Aleksandra's fiancé."

He reached out for the phone.

"What am I supposed to do with this?"

"There's a video on there you need to see."

He shook his head. I pulled the phone out and scrolled to the last recorded video on her phone. He pulled me toward a corner of the theater and watched the video. I didn't look at it, but I could hear it. I could imagine what was taking place as I heard the sounds of glass breaking and the coughing Aleksandra did as she tried to breathe her last breaths.

"Where's Sergei?"

"Yeah, I definitely need him to translate this, but you can see Anna and Irina in the background, and you can hear Aleksandra screaming. Plus with the time and date stamp from the phone, I can make a couple of arrests."

He smiled at me and leaned over to give me a kiss.

"Once again, my wife has mad crime solving skills I never knew. I'm signing you up for the police academy after we come back from Edisto. Go home and pack our bags."

He took out his phone and faced the corner. There was a rumble of noise in the theater. It made it difficult to hear. I strained to overhear what Drew was saying. I did make out the name "Irina," so I guessed he was sending someone to arrest her. I knew what his next move was going to be as he ended the call and headed toward the backstage dressing room area. I followed closely. I wasn't leaving until I saw it with my own eyes.

The dancers were dressed in their glorious tutus, waiting to go on. A few seamstresses stitched dancers into their dazzling costumes while other dancers jumped up and down to keep their muscles warm. The ballerinas glittered and shimmered; their bejeweled costumes reflecting the light. They were so beautiful. I wished I could stay for the performance, but what was about to transpire would definitely be more interesting.

I stood back as Drew marched toward Anna who was talking to one of the dancers. He motioned toward Sergei to follow him. He arrested her, and Sergei translated it into Russian so there would be no mistaking what was taking place.

The loud gasps and the conversation amongst the dancers drowned out the rest of Drew's statements and Sergei's translations. Anna looked just as shocked as they did as Drew led her out. I wondered where Irina was, but she'd be behind bars soon enough.

It was almost anticlimactic as I stood and watched. I thought it might be more interesting to see my husband put handcuffs on someone and arrest them. I wondered what rights she had as a Russian citizen on American soil, but I figured I'd let them sort that out. Irina, however, was an American citizen.

As I watched the commotion, one of the dancers broke from the rest and came toward me. It was Elena.

"My brother found you?" she asked, smiling broadly.

"Yes, he did."

She hugged me.

"Aleksandra was a beautiful dancer and a beautiful person. She wasn't a monster. She just wanted everything to be perfect."

"And your brother?"

"He's heartbroken."

"What's his name?"

She smiled.

"I must get on stage."

Despite the commotion, the dancers filed through the stage doors into the theater's wings. Although they probably wanted to see what was going on, they didn't miss their cues. Elena gave me a quick kiss on both cheeks and rushed through the doors with the rest of them.

I took that as my sign to leave too. I walked outside the theater to see Drew and Sergei talking. I guessed someone else had taken Anna away.

Drew walked over to me and put his arms around me.

"Have I told you how beautiful you are today?"

"No, you haven't."

"Well, you are."

"Thanks, but what happened on that video?'

"I thought you watched it since you knew exactly what I needed to find on the phone."

I wrinkled my nose.

"Only some of it. She seemed so happy at first."

"She was."

"She was talking to her fiancé about their upcoming wedding, and how much she missed him," Sergei interjected. "Kissy faces. Something about everything going to plan. They were going to be married next month. It wasn't going to be a big wedding. They'd planned on getting married at a beach in Greece."

"And that's where it got confusing. Irina and Anna came in," said Drew.

I wasn't sure I was following what was going on.

"What difference did it make to them whether she left the company or not?"

"Apparently, there was more going on with this company than

dance."

"I don't understand."

"I'm not sure either," said Drew. "They kept talking about some kind of merchandise they needed. Without her, there would be no more merchandise. With no product, no money. She was a traitor to them and to their country."

I shook my head.

"Killing her was stupid, but they didn't mean to. You could tell from their shock at the end of the video. They were only trying to scare her, threaten her, but they snapped her neck," said Drew.

"They talked about it after she was dead. Irina said it was all a mistake," said Sergei.

I remembered Emmie's message.

"Drew, have you talked to Special Agent Monroe lately?"

"I haven't checked my messages. Why?"

"Emmie left me a voicemail message that Aleksandra's fiancé was wanted for questioning about some type of European smuggling operation. She didn't know exactly what he was wanted for, and she said they thought that he was here illegally."

Drew pulled out his phone and scrolled through his messages.

"I didn't see this earlier. I have a missed call and voicemail from Frank Monroe. We aren't done here."

He walked a few feet away from me. I guessed it was habit to keep his conversation private, but I was going to eavesdrop anyway. Or at least try to eavesdrop. He wasn't keeping any secrets from me. I followed him.

"Hey, Frank, just got your message."

I wondered what the message was. I guessed it was similar to what Emmie had told me - that the mystery man was a smuggler of some sort. I wished I knew more about Russia. What would they be smuggling? I'd thought the whole situation was strange. Having two performances of a show at the Bell was odd. People typically didn't come in town for more than a night, and then discovering there's a huge Russian population only two hours away in Atlanta. Vladimir was really concerned about the Russian contingent in the audience. He didn't seem to care any for the locals. Then there was the whole adding of the show. People typically didn't do that either. I looked at Drew who continued to move away and was now pacing as he spoke to Agent Monroe. There was a lot of money wrapped up in these performances. I knew by the size of my paycheck. I'd planned on giving Jazzy and Emmie some extra money.

I glanced at Sergei. Did he know anything else about what was taking place? I walked over to him.

"Sergei, what's going on?"

He shook his head.

"I'm not sure."

"What else did Irina and Anna say to Aleksandra?"

"That if she left, they would lose money. She would cost them everything. She could not leave. They were trying to scare her into giving up her lover and not leaving the company. She didn't want to listen. She said she loved Philippe, and they would be married. She was done with them and their business - whatever that meant. That was the last thing she said. She screamed and then she said nothing. Anna scolded Irina because Irina held the ribbons tightly around Aleksandra's neck while Anna pushed her to the floor."

"So leaving the ballet company would make her a traitor, I suppose?" I asked as I recalled the word scrawled in red lipstick on the mirror.

Although the sun had begun to set, I could see the anguish in Sergei's eyes. I don't think he'd been prepared for what he'd seen on the video. I could understand that. I didn't watch the end. I couldn't watch someone die. I hope that he didn't see all of it. I wasn't sure how much was captured on video when she dropped her phone.

Most of the crowd had funneled into the theater by now. The performance would be starting soon. There was an awkward silence between Sergei and me as we waited for Drew to make his phone calls. I didn't know what to say to him. It seems like he got more on his student exchange than he'd signed up for. Out of the corner of my eye, I could see someone approaching us. I guess I shouldn't have been surprised that it was Beth. She loved stuff like this, and I didn't think she hadn't gotten to see the opening night because of Aleksandra's death.

She really was beautiful. She wore a strapless, knee length black dress with some sky high heels. That wasn't the same black dress I'd seen her in a couple of nights before. I wonder how many "little black dresses" she owned. She certainly used them with as many events and as many boards as she served on. Those shoes were amazing. They sparkled too, but there was no way I could walk in them without breaking an ankle or my neck. She seemed to float in them. Yes, there were times when I got jealous of Beth.

"Beth, what are you doing out here? Why aren't you inside?"

"Well, hello, Grace and Sergei. Fancy meeting you here," she smiled.

I shook my head.

"You knew we'd be here at some point."

"True. As for me, I was inside handing out some information on some upcoming events for next season for several of the arts groups I'm on the boards of. There's tons of stuff starting back up after the summer break. Besides, I saw the performance last night so I can miss the opening. Act 2 is not to be missed though. Aleksandra's replacement is amazing. She did this pique circle and then did at least 30 fouettes after that. I lost count. I've never seen anything like her. People were out of their seats cheering for her before she finished."

"I have no idea what that means."

Beth laughed.

"Basically, she spun around more than 30 times without stopping."

"And without throwing up?"

Beth nodded.

"Gotcha. That I understand."

"So did they arrest someone or not?"

"Yes, two people actually. And they may not be done."

"And you weren't going to tell me this?"

"I figured you'd read about it in the paper tomorrow," I said and laughed. "But the mystery isn't over. That's the reason we're still standing here."

I explained to her the events over the past hour, and I realized that flower arrangement was still where I'd left it at the shop. I wondered if there would be a party after all of this.

"I know Drew called Agent Monroe, but I'm sure he's not still on the phone with him."

"I wonder what your FBI agent friend has to say about all this."

"I'm wondering too. Emmie said that Aleksandra's fiancé was a smuggler, and Sergei said her killers were talking about merchandise. I wonder what they were bringing into the U.S."

Beth thought for a moment, and then her mouth dropped.

"I know exactly what the merchandise was. Grace, did you see the dancers' costumes?"

"Oh yes, they were beautiful and glittery."

"But some are more glittery than others, don't you think?"

"I didn't really notice."

"What do you want to bet that those weren't rhinestones but diamonds?"

"Diamonds?"

"Definitely diamonds," said Beth.

"I don't understand."

"My dear Grace, I know diamonds so let me school you in them."

"Okay?" I wasn't sure I wanted a lesson in diamonds, but she was going to tell me anyway. There was no stopping her. Beth truly believed the saying that diamonds were a girl's best friend.

"Russia is a huge producer of synthetic diamonds as well as mining natural diamonds. The country is responsible for about 20 percent of the diamonds in the world economy. In 2012, it was announced that there was this huge diamond mine in Siberia that had been formed when an asteroid hit the earth and made the Popigai crater millions of years ago. It literally has trillions of carats of diamonds in it. The Popigai crater is located in the Arctic Circle and at one time it was thought to be volcanic."

I nodded as I listened to her story, wondering what it had to do with anything.

"Let's just say the mine is hard to get to. It's in a remote area. Although the government has known about it for some time, it hasn't been economical for it to exploit the mine for its resources."

"And you think the diamonds have come from there?"

"I don't know, but there's been concern in the diamond market that these gems would cause instability because of the sheer amount of them."

"It's always about money, isn't it?"

"We all know that diamonds can be extremely expensive. I sat back and watched Natasha spin, and I wondered about her sparkle. I wonder if those diamonds from that crater have made their way onto the market."

"But wouldn't it be stupid to parade the diamonds in front of a whole bunch of people like that? And why would you put them in costumes?"

"No one is going to think twice about diamonds in the costumes. And no one would think they were real except for the person buying them. Maybe they wanted to see the merchandise before buying it. Those diamonds would definitely shine brighter than any rhinestones. Maybe it was a tantalizing appetizer for whoever is fencing the stones."

"And getting them through customs, who is going to question a flashy ballet tutu? You could put millions of dollars in diamonds in the costumes with no one being any wiser," Drew interjected. He was finally off the phone with Agent Monroe and whoever else he'd talked to.

"And really, who is going to think of Augusta as a place to smuggle diamonds to? It's the perfect place because they think no one will be looking for that. And we know that there are a lot of people from out of town here. You said they insisted on having the other performance. Their deal was going down this weekend. They couldn't postpone it. Wow, what an enterprise and what a cover," Beth said.

I nodded. My head was swimming. An international murder and a diamond smuggling operation. Even that was a little much for me in my sweet little hometown. I wouldn't have believed it if I hadn't seen it with my own eyes.

"But why Natasha's costume? Wouldn't it have been Aleksandra's costume? Those two couldn't have worn the same costume."

"The program listed Natasha as a soloist in one of the numbers. She had her moment in the spotlight even though Aleksandra was the principal soloist."

"And then there was Aleksandra's tiara that was missing from her dressing room. Who knows how many diamonds could have been in that tiara?"

"It all makes sense now," said Drew.

"Do you think Vladimir was in on the diamond smuggling too?"

"Babe, I have no idea, but I will be asking him some more questions, trust me on that. Beth, I owe you a steak dinner," said Drew. "Babe, I'll see you later today or maybe in the morning. I have a diamond smuggler to catch."

"Glad to be of help, Drew," Beth smiled.

"Sergei." Drew motioned for him to follow.

"Drew, wait, you need to talk to Elena. She's in with the mystery man."

"Why do you say that?"

"Our mystery man told me she was his half sister."

By now, it was dark. The performance was well underway in the time we'd stood outside. The parking lot was well lit, however. As I glanced up, there was a woman coming out of the side door of the Bell. She was carrying a garment bag, and she seemed to be struggling with it. It was Elena. I didn't recognize her at first because her hair was down, and she was wearing a baseball cap. Why wasn't she on stage? A car pulled up to the side door.

"Stop, police," Drew yelled and started to run toward the car.

Elena got into the back seat, and the car lurched backwards and attempted to speed out of the parking lot from the direction it came in. Drew had his weapon in hand and fired two shots, blowing out one of the tires. He fired again and hit the other back tire. The driver tried to keep moving, but soon the car ground to a halt. By the time Drew arrived at the car, several other deputies had raced out of the Bell Auditorium to his aid. Sergei, Beth, and I watched as Drew pulled the driver out of the car. It was Irina Meadows. I guess she hadn't gotten the news yet that her sister was in jail. I moved closer to the car - as close as they'd let me that is. I watched as they pulled Elena out of the back seat. And then, they pulled out the garment bags and unzipped them. Ballet costumes with diamonds, I guessed. Beth was right.

Beth had appeared behind me.

"Well, would you look at that? I think Shakespeare summed up Irina's threats by saying the 'lady doth protest too much.'"

"That's for sure, Beth. I wonder what all the squawking about them coming here was about."

"I know. She's apparently not the brightest crayon in the box."

"Well, I'd love to stay and watch all this go on, but I've got an after party to take flowers to."

Beth smiled.

"Let me help. Our work here is done."

# 12

I got to the shop early the next morning and stopped to get a copy of the newspaper on the way. There was a photo of my husband working the crime scene on the front page. I was proud of him, but I smiled mainly because I knew that Beth had taken the photo with the camera on her phone. It turned out well despite the fact that it was dark outside.

The after-party wasn't exciting at all. Most of the major players were dead or behind bars. Vladimir was there and Natasha. He was there for a while, anyway. Drew took him in for more questioning.

The party was awkward mainly because the people who were supposed to be at the party were probably the potential diamond buyers. Apparently, neither Vladimir nor Natasha had any knowledge of the diamond smuggling. I could believe it about Natasha, but I didn't buy it when it came to Vladimir. I think he knew more than what he was telling.

There was a lot of confusion concerning Aleksandra and the mystery man. Did she know he was a diamond smuggler? Was he using her to get diamonds into the U.S. and other countries? The murder left more questions than answers. And they didn't recover the tiara.

After Beth and I delivered the flowers, I went home to my sweet little cottage and sat on the steps of the porch. I leaned back on the column and stared at the stars, and all of the emotions rushed to the surface. The two dead young women and the total lack of compassion I'd witnessed over the past several weeks. I was tired, and I couldn't hold back the tears any longer. I'd tried to be strong for everyone, but now, alone, I could be me.

I thought about the God who made the stars I was gazing at, and I knew that if He cared for them, He cared for me too. He made sure they shined brightly in the night sky and gave them their beauty.

In my crying, I couldn't get out too many words. I couldn't pray, but He could hear the condition of my heart. He knew what I couldn't say. I felt the tsunami of emotions crashing through my shaking body as I wept. And then, just like that, it stopped. I felt relaxed and at peace with everything. I'm sure that wouldn't be the only time I'd cry or get emotional about what I'd seen, but it was a start.

I whispered a "thank you," and I sent a text to my pastor. I told him I needed someone to talk to, and he sent me back a message saying that he or anyone on staff would be able to talk to me whenever I was ready. With that, I knew I'd be able to rest. I went inside and passed out from exhaustion. I was asleep before Drew had made it home so I didn't get a chance to talk with him, and he was gone before I got up. I had to drag myself into work.

It looked like it was going to be a quiet weekend at my shop, and I was thankful for that. After all the excitement, I needed something routine or even bordering on dull. There were a couple of weddings scheduled, but Jazzy had taken care of the boutonnieres and bouquets already. Emmie was going to come in for a little while to work on some of the main arrangements for the altar and the reception. The two brides I'd dealt with were as far from bridezillas as possible, so I was hoping that was a good sign that all would go smoothly.

I enjoyed the quiet of the morning. I had some paperwork to finish. Around 10:45, I looked at the clock. Emmie was late. She was supposed to have been in at 10:30, and Jazzy was coming in after lunch. That wasn't like Emmie at all. Despite her free-spirited personality, she was amazingly punctual. I checked my phone - no messages. While I debated on whether to call her or the hospital to see if she was in the ER, I heard her coming in the back door.

When I saw her, I smiled, but at the same time, I wanted to cry.

Emmie was wearing a black hat with an enormous black and white polka-dotted bow. It was the one we'd seen in the back corner of the display window at Bing's. It had a huge brim, and it looked so cute with her short black dress with its flowing skirt. She looked like Audrey Hepburn. But I knew what that hat meant. Emmie had gotten the job.

"Well, what do you think about my hat?"

I smiled.

"Emmie, you rock that hat."

I got up and gave her a big hug. I think I held on a little too long.

"Don't cry, Grace, or I'll be in a puddle on the floor with you," she said, wiping tears from her eyes. "This isn't the end."

Before I could say anything else, I heard other voices. Beth was coming in the front of the shop with Drew following a few steps behind her.

"And to think I was that close to $30 million worth of diamonds," said Beth as she glanced at the newspaper that was lying on the counter.

"That's a lot of money," said Emmie. "I'd be happy with a diamond that cost $1,000."

"Oh Emmie, I love that hat," said Beth. "That would go perfect with $30 million in diamonds."

I smiled.

"Good morning, ladies," said Drew holding a large box from the Cupcakery.

"What is that?" I asked. I knew the answer, and I didn't give him time to say anything as I took the box from him and set it on the counter. Emmie and Beth both swarmed around it.

"You aren't going to let me say anything?" he asked.

"Nope," Beth answered.

"Do you have one of their chocolate chip cheesecake ones in there?" Emmie asked as she picked one up and looked at it.

"It's too early in the morning for all this sugar," I said.

"Hush your mouth," said Beth. "It's never too early for the Cupcakery."

"This is to thank you ladies for all of your input on this case," he said.

"They need a lemon pound cake one like my mother makes," I said. "Those would be heavenly."

"I got you one of the peanut butter ones you like so much," Drew said.

I walked over to him and gave him a quick kiss.

"I saw your picture on the front page," Beth interjected.

"And I wonder where they got it from?" he raised his eyebrow and looked at her.

"Camera phones are amazing with the detail they get, especially when you are zooming in from a distance."

"I've heard," he said, and he looked at me.

"I didn't take any photos last night. I promise, honey."

"And the others?"

"I deleted those."

"Good."

"Whatever happened to the mystery man? And what was his name?"

"Philippe Bertrand. And he's still a mystery man. I don't know where he is. We sent the sketch to a few of the hotels where we thought he might be. He was staying on the river, and the hotel staff identified him. He had a fake ID and was using the name Alexei Petrovich, the son of Peter the Great, a 17th century Russian czar. Alexei was executed at the age of 28 for plotting treason."

"Treason? That's interesting considering that was the message on the mirror."

"Very, but there's not much else to go on. I've been in contact with our FBI friends and they've issued BOLOs for him. He apparently uses several aliases. Elena has clammed up all of a sudden. She's very angry probably because her brother is on the outside, and she's not. Irina and Anna each blame the other one for the most part. That has been interesting because they've been telling on one another. Vladimir was clueless about the smuggling, but he did have some interesting things to tell, and Natasha just wanted to dance. I don't think we'll ever know what's really going on with this case. Too many questions and not enough answers."

"Do you think Philippe or whatever his name is is the one smuggling the diamonds?"

"He's definitely suspicious, and we never recovered that tiara."

All of a sudden I was sad. I wondered if Philippe had used Aleksandra to move the diamonds and didn't love her at all.

"What's wrong, babe?"

"She loved him so much. I could tell. I wonder if he loved her or if he was just using her?"

"That's another question I'm not sure I know the answer to. I was trying to solve a murder case not crack a ring of diamond smugglers."

"Well, less than two months ago, you were trying to catch a killer and ended up cracking a human trafficking ring. You seem to have a knack for these things."

He smiled.

"You had a lot to do with it too."

"Not just her," said Beth.

"No, all three of you," he said. "I did find out that the reason Irina raised such a big stink a few months ago about boycotting the ballet. Anna had let it slip to her sister about their sideline operation, and Irina wanted in on it. At first, they said 'no,' but Augusta was a key location for them. Irina pitched a fit earlier on, but when they paid for her to be quiet, she was quiet. But through her contacts, she sweetened the pot and found other Russians in the Southeast who were interested in the product. They wanted this to be a bigger operation and were planning on something better for next season."

"Wow, all this is amazing, but you're right. There are definitely more questions than answers Drew," Emmie chimed in.

"Yes, it's going to take a while to sift through this one, but presumably there were a few potential buyers at last night's performance. We think we know who they were. They were high on the 'sponsor' list. Whoever ponied up the most money got the first bid on the diamonds."

"Well, you did find out a few things after all," I was still curious though.

"A few things. Vladimir didn't know all that was going on, but he knew there was something different about this performance. He was surprised at all the money being thrown around too. He said it didn't happen in other cities except for Aleksandra's flowers. There was one donor who came through every time. I think that was Philippe. He told us who the money people were behind this show. We think there was going to be an auction at last night's after party, and the highest bidder got the diamonds."

"But Philippe knew he wouldn't get his cut, so he took the tiara?" I queried.

"It's possible."

"I still don't understand why they had to kill her."

"Money makes people do horrible things. And with Aleksandra leaving the ballet company to marry Philippe; the two of them could take the money and run and ruin Anna and Irina's future plans."

"What's going to happen with all of this? You've got foreign suspects and a foreign murder victim on American soil. Philippe said he was French, but I'm not sure I really believed all of his story."

"It's a mess that I don't have to worry about. I did my part. I arrested two murder suspects and a third person with a bunch of smuggled diamonds. With all the charges against them and two countries involved, I have no idea how it will play out or how long it will all take. Something like this won't be sorted out overnight."

"Wow, that's insane to think it all happened here," said Emmie.

"Yes, it sounds like we've given Frank Monroe more business," I added.

"As a matter of fact, Frank is on the way down here. Some of this will be his mess now."

"Well, I think the three of us make a great crime fighting team. Chalk up two wins for the girls," said Emmie. "And these cupcakes are heavenly, Drew. Thank you."

"We are good at this crime solving thing," interjected Beth. "I think Grace needs to convert that extra storage area in the back to an office, and we'll call this Grace's Flowers and Detective Agency."

She laughed.

"I'm hanging up my detective cap. I'm done. I've had enough dead bodies to last me a lifetime. Drew and I are going out of town next week, and I'm going to enjoy nature at Edisto Beach."

I tried to smile, but it was hard. When I got back, Emmie wouldn't be at my shop. She'd be on her next adventure, working as a sketch artist and doing something with graphics.

She walked around and gave me a big hug. It was almost like she could read my mind. When she did, her hat fell off. It was hard to hug someone wearing a hat that wide. She laughed, and I tried to. I wasn't being selfish with Emmie. I'd lost one friend due to that, and I wasn't making that same mistake this time.

"Grace, crime fighting is in your blood now. You can't deny it," she said trying to make a joke. "And what Beth said might not be a bad idea. You can let Jazzy do all the flowers for you. Give her a promotion and a raise, and you take over the detective part of the business."

"You can do the work for all three of us, Emmie. You have fun on your next adventure, solving crimes and putting bad guys behind bars."

"I'll be back. It's only a temporary position, and I need to touch flowers and leaves and put them into their place in foam and in vases. I need to smell roses. I can't get through a day without it."

I nodded and wiped a few stray tears away.

"No crying. You're my best friend. A job is never going to take that away. We were friends before you opened your shop, and we'll be friends the day you retire from it," Emmie said. "And now after this delicious cupcake, I've got a flower arrangement to make. Jimmy and Peggy Hughes' anniversary is tomorrow, and I think he had something special in mind."

I smiled. I'd forgotten about Jimmy's order, but I was glad Emmie had not.

"Jimmy is my best customer, and I've stocked accordingly."

"Good. We should keep him out of the doghouse at least one day out of the year."

Lottie Lou's Luscious Lemon Pound Cake

½ pound (2 sticks) butter, softened
½ cup shortening
3 cups sugar
5 eggs
1 tsp vanilla
3 cups all-purpose flour
½ tsp salt
½ tsp baking powder
2/3 cup milk
1/3 cup lemon juice
1-2 tbsp. lemon zest
Preheat oven to 350 F.
Grease and flour Bundt pan.

Mix flour, salt, and baking powder together. Set aside. With a mixer, cream butter and shortening together, add sugar, 1 cup at a time. Add eggs, 1 at a time, beating after each addition. Add vanilla. Mix milk, lemon juice, and lemon zest together. Add flour and liquid mixture in an alternating pattern, starting with flour and ending with flour. Pour into Bundt pan and bake for 1-1&½ hours until toothpick inserted in center comes out clean.

If you enjoyed Murder En Pointe, please consider leaving a review at Amazon. The third book in Grace' Augusta Mystery Series is Murder Makes the Ballot.

Also, you may enjoy Charmain's Victoria James Mystery Series beginning with Murder at Twin Oaks. It's available on Amazon.

https://www.amazon.com/dp/B00MUC5JE8

Sign up for more books news by subscribing to her newsletter at czbblog@gmail.com.

Find her on Facebook at www.facebook.com/thekeyofelyon or on Twitter @CZBrackett.